Haunted Past

Firehouse Blues Series: Book 5

AE Moran

Invisible Publishing Company

Firehouse Blues Series

Contents

Chapter 1: Brooke

A deafening blast echoes through the firehouse and all the fire-fighters and paramedics take off running for their vehicles. I jump in the back seat of the rescue truck with Josh Abbott.

Keith Brewer hits the gas and pulls the truck out onto the street with the lights flashing and the siren blaring. The ladder truck and two ambulances pull out right behind us.

"What do we got?!" Keith yells to Billy Cates in the seat next to him.

Danny Brewer, Caleb Watts, and Ellis Barrett crowd into the seat behind them and we all scramble to finish putting on our turnouts on our way to the call.

Billy checks the dispatch notes on the truck's dashboard computer. "Fire in an office tower downtown! Twenty people unaccounted for. Everyone else made it out."

"Does it say how many patients?" I yell over the seat.

"Fifty employees on the ground!" he calls back. "No word yet of their injuries or even if there are any injuries."

"This should be fun!" Ellis chirps.

"Keep your pants on, Slappy," Billy snaps over his shoulder. "Just watch out for the.....holy shit!"

We all jump as Fire Chief John Brewer burns past us in his bright red support pickup. He motors ahead of the rescue truck and clears the way of all traffic.

We come to an intersection with a red light, but John's truck is already there with its lights and sirens wailing, too. He parks in the center of the intersection to make sure no traffic enters. The rescue truck can drive right on through.

John keeps jumping intersections and stopping traffic for us until we get to the scene.

We don't have to look too far to find the burning building. A column of black smoke billows from its windows and roof. We spot the smoke cloud miles away.

The Police have set up roadblocks for a dozen city blocks around the building. Uniformed officers let the truck through and Billy cuts the siren.

"Pull your truck over there," one of the Police officers tells Keith through the driver's window.

"Won't we need to get closer to use the ladder?" Keith asks.

"You won't be able to. You don't have a ladder long enough to get the trapped people down."

"What do you mean?" Keith asks. "I don't understand."

"Just park your truck and I'll show you. Fire Chief Brewer is over there talking to Police Chief Walker right now."

Keith mutters under his breath and pulls the truck over to where the officer indicated. "I guess we just have to find out what this is all about. Let's go."

We all jump out and follow Keith and Billy to the building, but the officer is right. We couldn't have gotten the truck in here.

We meet up with John and Police Chief Jim Walker. "The trapped people are up there." Chief Walker points to the top of the building.

"We know they're there because they got a window open and waved for us to come and get them. None of your ladders are long enough to reach that high, so we're sending up a crane to get them."

"Do you know the situation inside?" John asks. "Have you been able to communicate with anyone by cellphone?"

"We got a 911 call half an hour ago. They have injured patients up there—and all twenty of the missing employees are in one spot. You can send up your people in the crane bucket and get them out."

John takes a look at the crane. The bucket on the end is six feet square. "Okay, we'll have to leave plenty of room for the patients. We'll send up one firefighter and one paramedic. Brooke and Billy, you can go. If we need more people, we'll send them up. The rest of you spread out and start triaging the employees who are already on the ground. Let's go."

He escorts me and Billy to the crane. We have to climb another ladder to get inside the crane bucket. I take my drug box and Billy takes the rescue truck jump kit.

It isn't ideal that we're taking so little gear, but we won't be able to treat any patients up there anyway. Our only mission is to get them out of the building.

Billy and I climb into the bucket and John hands Billy a two-way radio. "Take this. You'll be able to communicate with the crane operator and tell him where to position the bucket and when to bring you down."

Billy nods. "Got it."

"Put these safety straps around your waists and clip yourselves to the bucket safety rail. You, too, Brooke. The patients won't be able to, but we don't want to risk you falling out."

He shows us how to buckle ourselves in. Then John climbs down and Billy shoots me a grin. "Hold onto your panties, sweetheart. We're going up."

I grin back at him, but right then, the bucket clunks when the crane arm unlocks from the truck.

Huge outriggers support the truck on both sides and the arm starts to extend. The bucket rises farther and farther above the ground. John, Chief Walker, and everyone else get smaller and farther away.

I don't want to look down, so I look up at the building instead. I can't see where the trapped people are from here, but as soon as I look up, someone sticks their head out of a window and waves. They're on the thirty-fifth floor.

"Damn," Billy mutters under his breath. "It's a good thing I'm not afraid of heights or this call would put me in a coma."

I don't answer. I've never been afraid of heights before, but this is definitely the first time I've ridden in a crane bucket thirty-five floors off the ground.

I don't have time to get scared. The bucket keeps rising. The trapped employees get more desperate and frantic as we get closer. A couple different people stick their heads out and we hear them yelling at us.

"Looks like they really, super-duper want to go home," Billy remarks. "Time to ride to the rescue."

He gets on the two-way radio with the crane operator. "Up a little more. Move us closer to the building. Stop!"

The bucket bangs against the window. We can't see inside with all the people crowding around the open window.

"Calm down, everyone!" Billy orders in his big, deep, booming voice. "Quit shoving! We're going to get you all out! Just calm down and back away so I can get in. Back off, everyone! We need to get inside to give your injured colleagues medical attention."

It takes a while for the employees to get the message. They finally ease off enough for Billy to climb inside. Then he turns around to take the drug box from me, puts it on the floor, and grabs me to help me climb through the open window.

He has to stand there and make sure the trapped employees stay calm enough to climb one at a time into the crane bucket.

"Spread out through the room and find the injured patients!" he yells at me over the noise of a dozen people all talking at once. "I'll deal with this."

He holds back everyone pushing and shoving toward the window. He has to help most of the employees climb onto the windowsill and into the bucket.

Only ten people will fit in the bucket at a time and that's with them jammed in tight against each other.

"You have to wait for the next load!" Billy tells the others. "Just stay calm! Back off!" He gets on the radio. "Take it down. The first load of employees is coming down."

That leaves me to go through the room and check the patients. I don't have any problem finding them, either. They're the only people not crowding the window trying to get the hell out of here.

As soon as I pass all the employees shoving to get into the bucket, I also find out why they're all so desperate to leave. We're in a conference room with flames chewing through the back wall.

Smoke boils from under the door, crawls up the walls, and covers the ceiling. Fire eats its way through whole back wall of the room, but the fire doesn't break through completely—not yet.

The trapped employees keep casting terrified glances over their shoulders. They burst out in fresh shoving and yelling every time they see the flames.

Telling Billy how bad the situation is won't make the crane move any faster.

I cross to the other side of the room. Four people sit apart from the crowd and one big man lies sprawled on the ground.

I check his pulse. It feels normal and he's breathing okay. His skin color looks good, too. I can't tell right away what's wrong with him.

A woman in a business suit with her hair messed up sits in the opposite corner. She presses a bloodstained handkerchief to her forehead.

A man in a suit hunches next to her with his arm jammed tightly against his ribs. His hair falls in his eyes and he pants for breath while his eyes dart around the room. He must have broken some ribs.

The other two patients are a middle-aged woman and a ten-year-old boy. She sits with her arm around his shoulders and I can see right away that he has a broken leg.

I don't see anything wrong with her. She must be his mother. She's only sitting down to stay near him and comfort him.

I go over to them. "I'm Brooke Elsworth. I'm a paramedic with the Howe County Fire Department. We're going to get you out, okay? Let me take a look."

I pull the woman's handkerchief away. She has a big gash across her hairline, but it isn't bleeding anymore.

I push her hand back up. "Keep holding pressure on it. It doesn't look too serious. You'll be at the hospital soon and they'll stitch it up." I turn to the man with the broken ribs. "Are you holding on okay, Sir? Can you hold out long enough to get in the crane bucket? We have ambulances waiting for you on the ground."

"I'm fine," he pants. "Just get us the hell out of here."

I nod. "We will." I glance over at Billy. He's on the two-way radio and looking out the window.

I hear him say, "The crane is on the way back up."

I glance the other way at the flames. Heat radiates into the room. We don't have much time, but I have to stay calm for these people.

I get the jump kit and pull out a few splints for the boy's leg. "This is the best we can do until we get you to an ambulance. Getting out of the building is going to hurt, but it's better than staying here, right?"

He looks up at me with huge, petrified eyes and then they dart toward the flames. He nods. "Yeah. It is."

I strap the splint around his leg. "Just hold on a little longer. We're getting all of you out of here."

The bucket clunks against the building. The other employees shove and yell to get into the bucket.

One man keeps yelling, " "Take us down! Take us down!"

"Not yet!" Billy yells back. "We still have space for the others. Come on, Brooke!"

I grab the woman with the wound on her scalp. "Get in the bucket! You, too, Sir. Come on, Ma'am. Get in the bucket! I'll get your son."

The man and the woman with the scalp wound get up immediately. Billy helps them clamber into the bucket. The mother won't leave her son. I have to push her away. "Go! I got him!" I turn to the boy. "Here we go! Just hold on!"

I see his face twisting in fear of the pain that's about to come, but I can't wait. I scoop him up in my arms.

He screams out in pain and his mother turns back. "Franklin!!"

Billy has to physically lift her over the windowsill. "Get in!" he bellows.

I carry the boy still screaming to the window. Billy takes him off my hands and pushes him into his mother's arms. The boy's shrieks echo off the surrounding tower walls.

"Take 'em down!" Billy roars into the radio. "Take 'em down!"

The bucket starts moving away from the building. I turn back to the big man lying on the floor. I have to crawl toward him so I don't suffocate in the smoke and heat.

A thick layer of smoke covers the ceiling now. I can barely see the flames with so much smoke choking the room.

"What's wrong with him?!" Billy yells at me.

"I don't know! We don't have time to work on him here!"

I seize two fistfuls of the patient's jacket. It takes all my strength to drag him closer to the window. He's too heavy for me to lift.

I grab my jump kit. I have a few minutes before the bucket comes back. Billy and I will just have to hold out until then.

Billy springs across the conference room and wrenches a fire extinguisher off the wall. I didn't notice before. The other employees must not have noticed it, either.

The fire extinguisher is too close to the flames. Billy yanks on his heavy leather gloves, but he still almost drops the fire extinguisher when he tries to grab it.

"Aargh!" he yells and the fire extinguisher falls on the floor. He manages to catch it between his boots and hold it there so it doesn't fall over.

He shakes out his hands, rips out the pin, and aims the fire extinguisher toward the flames. They're already crawling onto the floor toward us.

I can't tell if the spray does any good, but it's better than nothing. I bend over the patient and check his pupils.

One of them looks normal. The other is blown wide open. I can't see any color at all. That explains what's wrong with him. He must have a head injury, but I can't see any injuries from the outside.

I wouldn't be able to do anything if I could see an injury.

Billy's voice snaps my head up real quick. "The bucket is here!" he yells over his shoulder. "Get him up and let's get out of here!"

"I can't lift him!" I jump up and race over to Billy. "You put him in the bucket! I'll cover you!"

I grab the fire extinguisher out of his hands. It's been away from the fire long enough for the handle to cool.

I don't try to lift the fire extinguisher off the floor. I drag it backward toward the patient and unload the spray on the advancing flames.

Billy hoists the patient into a fireman carry over his shoulder. The patient is so big even Billy strains under his weight. "Aargh!" Billy roars again. "Come on, Brooke!"

Billy rushes the window, slings one leg over the windowsill, and starts climbing into the bucket.

I unleash one more stream from the fire extinguisher and back away still unloading on the flames. I just have to dampen the fire long enough for all three of us to get into the bucket.

At that moment, a blast of backdraft explodes the conference room wall apart. An almighty fireball smashes into the room and knocks me off my feet.

I go flying and slam into the windows right next to the bucket.

"BROOKE!!" Billy roars.

He drops the patient in the bucket and springs back into the room to grab me. The fire licks closer to us, but now it rises up to the ceiling.

Billy pounces on me, seizes me in his arms, and picks me up. "I got you!" he keeps yelling. "I got you!"

I'm still dazed, but I feel that I'm not hurt. Billy doesn't take the time to check. He drags me to the window, picks me the rest of the way up, and climbs into the bucket still holding onto me. The patient lies on the floor in a pile.

"Get us down!!" Billy roars into the radio. "Take us down now! Get us out of here!"

The bucket moves away from the building and starts to descend, but right then, another explosion detonates the whole floor.

The conference room windows blast out. Billy dives on top of me and flattens me inside the bucket as broken glass and fire pelt over our heads. All that debris peppers the bucket, but it doesn't hit us.

"Are you okay?!" Billy yells at me. "Are you hurt?!"

"I'm okay!" I holler back. "I'm okay! Are you?"

"Yeah!" he yells. "We made it!"

I look up at him and he smiles. His blue eyes sparkle. We made it and we got everyone out of the building.

Chapter 2: Billy

Fire Chief John Brewer comes over to me and claps me on the shoulder. "You okay, man?" he asks.

I nod. "I'm fine. Things got kinda hectic up there, but we made it." I look past him. "Is Brooke okay?"

"She's fine. She says she didn't pass out, so we don't think she has a head injury. You two did great up there. I'm proud of you."

I bite back a grin. "We can still pull it off when we have to."

"You did more than that. You rocked it." He jerks his thumb toward the rescue truck. "You two are late to go off shift. Ride back to the firehouse with the rescue truck and go home. You've done your hero duty for one day."

I laugh, but he's already walking away. I don't want to go to the rescue truck until I see that Brooke is okay.

I walk over to the ambulance where Josh is checking her pupils for the hundredth time. "What's the prognosis, Doc?" I ask.

"She's gonna make it." He straightens up and sticks his pen light back in the chest pocket of his uniform. "You can go. You don't even have a concussion."

"I keep telling you that, but you won't listen." She stands up. She's still wearing her turnouts. None of the fire crew would let her take them off until Josh finished checking her out.

"John says we can go home," I tell her. "Keith is taking the rescue truck back to the firehouse. Let's go."

"Maybe I should stay and help with the rest of these patients." Her eyes dart to two dozen more employees who escaped from the same burning building.

"They're all walking wounded," Josh tells her. "We can handle it without you. Go home. We won't be here much longer anyway."

That finally convinces her. She heads for the rescue truck where Keith, Danny, Caleb, and Ellis are putting away all their gear.

They've been working to triage and transport all the patients from the building while Brooke and I were inside.

I find it hard to believe the world has been going on as normal while Brooke and I were up there. Time stopped up there. Now it's taking me some time to get things moving again.

"You okay?" she asks.

I look down to see her gazing up at me. She's so short she barely comes up to my shoulder. I can't see her wavy auburn hair pulled into a ponytail or her curvy body under her helmet and turnouts.

Soot smudges her face, but her clear green eyes shine out at me the way they always do. She always looks at me like that—like she actually cares about me. She's one of the only people I've ever met who always, ALWAYS looks at me like that.

"I'm okay," I tell her. "I was just worried about you."

She lays her slim, soft hand on my arm. I'm wearing a T-shirt so she winds up touching my skin. "I'm okay. Thank you for getting me out. You're my hero."

I snort with laughter. "Don't you start with that. You're the hero. You saved that boy and everyone else. I wouldn't have been able to get that big guy out without you."

She grins back at me. "Let's call it even. Come on. Let's go."

She stops by the truck to take off her turnouts. The guys are still working to put their stuff away, so we aren't leaving right away anyway.

She takes off her helmet, tosses it under the back seat, tidies up her hair, and then pulls off her jacket.

Her fire department T-shirt underneath is tight enough to show off her chest and narrow waist. Then she pushes down her turnout pants to reveal her round hips, muscular thighs, and tapering calves to her feet.

She's gorgeous enough to turn any man's head—and she does. Nothing like that could ever happen between us. We're too close, but the way she looks makes me protective of her. I don't want some jackass getting ideas and treating her wrong.

No one on the fire crew treats her that way, but outsiders do. They take one look at her body and magnetize to her like moths to a flame. Someone has to beat the morons off with a stick.

I wait for her to finish—and then the guys finish. We load up and go back to the firehouse.

The ambulance crews get back at the same time we do. We talk and joke around while we finish cleaning up our vehicles, restocking supplies, and getting ready to go off shift.

"Did you see that guy with the pen stain all over his shirt?" Ellis asks. "That sucker could NOT stop talking about his ruined shirt. He was more worried about his shirt than his colleagues."

Brooke turns to Josh. "Did you find out what happened to that big guy from the building?"

"He was going into surgery the last time we left the hospital," Josh replies.

"I'm surprised he made it. One of his pupils was completely blown."

"I saw that. You gave him his one chance at survival."

I put my arm around her shoulders and give her a side hug. "You hear that? I told you. You get today's hero badge."

She turns bright red. "You got the guy out of the building—not me. You got *me* out of the building, too."

"Aw! We can be heroes together." I kiss the side of her head. "How about we go out and celebrate tonight—just you and me? I'm buying."

She beams up at me. "Twist my arm."

Josh frowns at us and passes his forefinger back and forth between us. "Are you two....?"

"NO!!" Brooke and I both exclaim at the same time.

"We're very distantly related," she tells him. "I think we're fifth cousins or something. That's all."

I stick out my tongue. "Pew! That would be disgusting!"

"Disgusting?!" she fires back. "I would be disgusting?!"

"You know what I mean. It would be like dating my sister. I couldn't do that."

She laughs at me. "Watch it, pal."

Just then, John pulls in and gets out of his support truck. "If you two are feeling up to it, would you mind coming up to my office? I need you both to give me a report on everything that happened inside the building."

"You mean...both of us?" I ask.

"If you want to....or you could do it separately. It's up to you."

"We can go at the same time," Brooke replies. "I don't want to miss out on the free drinks."

We follow John upstairs to his office. I would be worried about John getting me in trouble if Brooke wasn't here.

John is the best boss I've ever had. He wouldn't call me to his office if I was in trouble—not without warning me first. He said he was proud of the way Brooke and I handled ourselves in the building.

Still, going to John's office always feels like going to the principal's office in grade school.

He's the nicest guy ever and beyond fair as a boss. He's also six inches shorter than I am and fifty pounds lighter, but he can intimidate anyone, even his brother Keith.

I hold the door open for Brooke to enter first—and not because I'm scared to face John. She smiles at me and we both pull up in front of John's desk.

He leans back in his desk chair—a sure sign that he's relaxed and this meeting is no big deal.

"So who wants to go first?" he asks.

Brooke launches into the whole story starting from when the crane bucket first left the ground. She goes through every detail right up until the end and doesn't leave anything out.

I listen in silence. She speaks so clearly and effortlessly. I would get seriously nervous if I had to explain something like that to John. She handles this so much better than I could.

John turns to me. "Do you want to add anything to that, Billy?"

"No," I reply. "That about covers it."

He leans forward and checks something on his computer. "One of the office guys is saying you delayed sending the second load of passengers to the ground. He says you put everyone in danger unnecessarily."

"He wanted us to lower the bucket when we still had room inside it!" I blurt out. "We got the last five able-bodied people on board, but there was still room for the four patients—I mean the *other* four patients—not that big dude. Whoever this idiot is who wants to complain would have left a man with broken ribs and a little boy with a broken leg inside the building—all to save his own skin!"

John turns to Brooke. "Is that what you saw, too, Brooke?"

She nods. "The guy panicked. He kept yelling for us to take him down, take him down. We had to load the four patients on board—and the boy's mother kept holding back. That's what delayed the trip. We sent the bucket down as soon as the four patients got on board. You can ask the other employees. They must have seen the same t hing."

John checks something else on his computer. "Actually, that is what they're saying. They all say the same thing—which is that you delayed getting the four patients on board. None of them have a problem with your actions."

"Then that settles it," Brooke finishes.

John nods. "You both did well. I'm impressed that you got the big guy out. Any lesser rescuer would have left him behind."

"We couldn't do that!" she insists.

"Like I said, you both did well. That was good thinking, Billy—going for the fire extinguisher. Obviously no one else thought of it."

His comments make me uncomfortable. "Was there something else you wanted to clarify about that call?"

"No, you two are done. You can go home."

We leave his office, but Brooke lays her hand on my arm to stop me in the hall outside. "Hey! Are you okay? That was no big deal. That guy's complaints don't mean anything."

I growl through clenched teeth. "The shithead doesn't even have the brains to be grateful to us for saving his sorry ass."

"You're right. He's an idiot. It doesn't mean anything. You heard what John said. All the other employees are vouching for us."

I look away. "Yeah."

"Do you still want to go out?" She swivels in front of me and smiles up at me. "We can find some way to take your mind off it."

I find myself smirking at her. "Twist my arm."

She breaks into a broader grin. "Let's go."

Chapter 3: Billy

I set two shot glasses on the bar in front of Brooke—right next to my beer and her marguerita.

She grabs her shot glass and tosses it back right away. "Slow down, girl," I tell her. "The night is young."

"You only live once." She takes another drink from her marguerita. "Do you want to shoot some pool—or darts?"

"You couldn't hit the broadside of the barn."

"Come on!" she tells me. "We're here to have a good time and drown our sorrows."

"You're gonna drown yourself. Then where will I be? I won't have you around to bail my ass out of trouble."

"Stop it. We aren't talking about that. Come on. I want to play pool."

She goes over to the pool table, puts some quarters in the slot, and pushes it in to get the balls. I take a swig of my beer and go over to join her.

I don't hold out much hope for this game, but I'll do whatever she wants to do. She's right that we're here to let our hair down and relax.

I catch plenty of guys in the bar checking her out on the side. She looks outstanding in a pair of fitted jeans and a tight black body suit with a cropped plaid blouse buttoned under her breasts.

Her clothes show off exactly what those guys are missing, but they don't come near her as long as I'm around. I have that effect on people.

She doesn't notice everyone scoping her out. She's completely oblivious to their attention.

That's the thing about her. She doesn't even know she's gorgeous. She thinks she's a tomboy who works for the fire department and never wears girly clothes.

She racks the balls, messes them up, and has to redo it a second time. I sit back and watch. I'm in no hurry to get this game started. I'm here to hang out with her—not to prove my manly billiard skills.

She racks and then breaks, but she doesn't sink anything. I'm just stepping up to the table to take my turn when she goes back to the bar to take another sip of her marguerita.

She grabs my shot glass while she's there and pounds it. "Hey!" I yell.

She laughs at me. I'm no chemist, but she's definitely showing signs of intoxication. "You snooze, you lose, baby."

"I can see I'm definitely going to be the one driving you home tonight, lightweight." I bend over and take my shot. I deliberately miss to make the game take longer.

She misses her next shot, but not on purpose. She brings her marguerita over, sits down on the stool next to me, and nods at my half-empty beer bottle. "Do you want another one?"

"Not if I'm driving both of us home." I frown at her. "What's gotten into you? You never drink like this."

"I don't know. Maybe that call today got to me more than I realized."

"You held up so well in John's office," I point out. "I couldn't have explained it the way you did."

"I mean the guy that complained. I guess I need to do something drastic to forget it."

I trace my thumb through the dewy drops on my beer bottle. I don't want to talk about it, but it looks like we're talking about it anyway. "He's an idiot."

"Like he couldn't hear that little boy screaming," she goes on. "I don't know if you saw the guy with the broken ribs, but he wasn't doing well, either. He was going pale. I wasn't even sure he would be able to walk or climb into the bucket." She looks up at me and her expression changes. "Are we somehow different from other people because we care enough to save people's lives? Is the rest of the world just not that interested in whether other people live or die?"

I don't know how to answer that. I've never talked to anyone at the firehouse about this. I would never dare to talk to anyone about it besides her.

"I don't want to believe that," I tell her. "In fact, I don't believe it. I don't think we're different. He's the one who's different. He's the one who doesn't care about other people."

She shrugs it away and takes another slug of her marguerita. "Anyway, like we told John, the guy panicked. Maybe he realized afterward that he was being a jerk."

"Why would he complain about it, then? He should have just crawled off into his hole to hide his face in shame."

She laughs and glances toward the table. "We aren't playing. It's your turn."

I take my shot, miss, and walk back over to her. "Let's get out of here. I don't feel like hanging around here anymore."

"Do you want to go somewhere else?" she asks. "It's only ten o'clock."

"I don't think so. I just want to crash. Come on. I'll drive you home."

She downs the rest of her marguerita before she follows me outside. Now I know she needs to erase that guy's complaint from her mind. She never drinks like this.

She stumbles on the stairs and falls against me. I catch her to steady her, but all that booze is catching up with her.

She doesn't even try to go back to her own car. I put her in the passenger seat of my truck and head across town to her place.

I stop at a red light and glance over at her. She leans her head against the window staring out at the streetlights. She looks.....sad. I can't remember ever seeing her so sad.

She doesn't move the whole way to her apartment. I don't expect her to stay conscious that long, but she perks up the minute I park. "Come inside!" she tells me. "I want to show you something."

"What is it?" I ask.

She grins. "You'll see."

She tries to get out, but she can't get the door open. I don't trust her to walk into the apartment, either. Her apartment is up three flights of stairs. She might fall and hurt herself in this condition.

I go around to the passenger door and help her get out. She staggers a lot more now and she starts talking a mile a minute as soon as she gets out of the cab.

"You should sign up for more training, Billy. You should get your EMT certification and become a paramedic......or sign up for leadership training. You could become a fire chief or at least a senior officer. You could move up in the ranks. You wouldn't have to stay down at the bottom of the ladder. Today proved you have the skills and leadership ability. You sell yourself short, but you're as good as Keith or Danny or Josh or anyone."

I don't answer. I'm not about to put myself in the same category as Keith Brewer and definitely not Josh Abbott. Those guys are pros. I'm just a firefighter.

The weird thing is that she doesn't slur her words. She knows exactly what she's saying....so why is she saying it?

She drops her keys when she tries to unlock her apartment. I hold her up with one arm, pick up her keys with my other hand, and unlock the door.

I flick on the lamp next to the couch to keep the light low. Her apartment isn't as fancy as some, but she keeps it neat with a big leather couch, mahogany coffee table, and two stained-glass lamps on either end.

I expect her to pass out on the couch if she even makes it that far.

Instead, she seems to come back to her senses the minute she gets inside. She stands up straight, crosses the living room to the bookshelf, takes something down, and brings it back.

"Sit down." She pulls me down on the couch.

I brace myself to find out what she's going to show me, but instead of just sitting there, she kicks off her shoes, curls her legs under her, and leans against me.

She winds up pushing me back against the cushions, putting her head on my shoulder, and cuddling up on the couch next to me.

I stiffen, but she doesn't mean anything by this. She's just drunk and wants someone to make her feel safe. I can do that.

She picks up whatever she's holding and raises it in front of my face. "See? Now do you understand?"

I look down at a framed newspaper clipping showing me, Keith, Danny, John, and four other firefighters who don't work at Howe Firehouse anymore.

The clipping includes a picture of us all being decorated for valor, heroism, and service after we saved forty people from a burning gymnasium. The Howe High School drama club was putting on a play when one of the stage lights shorted out and set a curtain on fire.

The call was almost exactly the same as today's except that the building was different. Almost the whole audience escaped just fine, but these people got trapped in one burning part of the building.

John, Danny, Keith, and I went in to get them out. We almost got trapped ourselves, but we got everyone out alive in the end.

So why does Brooke have this newspaper clipping framed in her apartment? She didn't even work at Howe Firehouse then.

Could she really care about me that much? She doesn't care about anyone else in that picture that much. She doesn't know half the people in it. She's never even met them.

The only other people in it she does know are the Brewer brothers. She wouldn't keep a newspaper clipping about them. That leaves me.

We've always been close since we first started working together. I didn't realize she cared this much.

"Everyone talks about the Brewers, but you're just as much a hero as they are," she tells me. "You could be like that. You're every bit as good as they are. You just have to believe it."

She nuzzles her forehead into my neck....and passes out completely. Her arm falls over my chest and the frame drops onto the carpet.

She's drunk enough that I could slip out of the apartment without waking her up, but I don't want to do that. I don't want to just abandon her.

I don't want her to walk up tomorrow morning feeling ashamed of what she did. She has every right to get plastered if something is bothering her.

I stare up at the ceiling. This sensation of her body against me—it does something to me.

I've hugged her a thousand times. I can't even remember all the times I've hugged her. I picked her up to get her out of the burning building. I've picked her up a million times.

I never thought anything about it before. I never think twice about hugging her or even kissing the side of her head. She's my friend—probably the one person on the fire crew I'm closest to.

Lying here with her like this—it feels different. It feels like....something more. Could it be?

She doesn't mean it as more. She doesn't mean it as anything, which means I can't think of it as that.

She sure does feel nice, though. I can't remember the last time I held a woman like this.

Actually, I can remember it, but I try not to. I push that thought away, but I can't push away the sensation of her breasts and stomach pressing against my chest and side, her arm lying across me, and one of her thighs draped over my leg.

I get a rush of sensation and emotion thinking about what it would be like if we were together for real.

What if she wasn't drunk right now but only asleep next to me? I could kiss her.....and turn her over.....and roll on top of her.....I could make her sigh....and moan.....and scream my name....

I turn my head away, but I can't get the thought out of my head.

I know exactly what she looks like. I know every tasty inch of her body—but only through her clothes. I never shied away from checking her out before.

I've been standing guard over her all these years. I want to make sure no one mistreats her or uses her....but what if I only did that because I want her for myself?

She isn't my sister even though we both say that. We both make a point of saying we could never get together because we're too close—but that obviously isn't the case. It can't be if I'm thinking of her like this.

Her voice shrieks in my ear. *Billy....oh God, Billy....I need you so bad! Please.....take me.....I need you....harder....oh, yes, harder.....Billy!*

I really need to stop thinking about that, but thinking about it starts to make me hard. She never has to know I fantasized about her like this. It can't do any harm because I won't ever act on it.

I drift into a hypnotic trance thinking about her breasts in my face, her thighs straddling my hips, and her sweet box pulsing around my throbbing shaft.

She doesn't stir when I slide my hand down inside my jeans and stroke myself.

Billy.....please.....yes.....harder.....! Oh, yes! Oh! Oh! Oh!

My fingers crushing her ass in both hands.....her thighs slapping against me as her juices run down my legs.....her fingers in my hair as she pulls my face into her chest.....her nipples going tight and hard in my mouth.......

I tense my body all over as I escalate to an explosion. I don't move except to contract my abs. She doesn't wake up. She'll never know.

Then the fantasy changes to her on all fours with me behind her. Her magnificent globe ass points up at me as I drive into her. She hurls herself back to slam into me taking it deep and hard and true. Oh, hell ye s.

Me running my hand up her spine to the back of her neck.....my fingers clenching in a fistful of her hair.....yanking her head back and making her scream as I hammer her to a gushing climax.....my jiz dripping out of her when I erupt into her.....her screams echoing in my ear as she begs me to take her harder......

I grit my teeth and swallow a groan when I unload into my boxers. I'll just have to lie here like this until morning, but the dreams floating in my head are too sweet for me to care.

I drift off thinking about us collapsing on the bed in a sweaty mess and kissing endlessly until we both get turned on enough to do it again.

Chapter 4: Brooke

I drift out of my coma and have to blink the glue out of my eyes before I realize where I am. I'm lying on the couch in my living room.

Billy lies next to me with my arms around him. My head rests on his chest. He's asleep.

I try to remember how we got here. Then I see the framed newspaper clipping lying on the carpet. I remember showing it to him....and then nothing.

Did something happen between us last night and I just don't remember it? Did we hook up?

Thinking that brings up a thousand other questions I've never asked myself before. Could there be anything between me and Billy?

Josh isn't the first person to ask. Billy and I have always been close, but we've both always insisted that it never went any further than friendship. It never has before.

But could it?

He isn't what anyone would call good-looking. He's big, burly, rough, gruff, and has a tendency to be on the abrasive side when he deals with other people. He's like Keith Brewer that way except that Keith actually does have some social skills.

Keith would never get as bent out of shape about some idiot on a call making a complaint about not getting rescued fast enough.

Then again, I shouldn't have gotten bent out of shape about that, either. I should have let it roll off. I shouldn't have needed to get shitfaced drunk to forget it.

Billy's size and protective nature always make me feel safe. I never have to worry about him—ever.

If we did hook up, he would have been careful and made sure I had a good time. The fact that he's still here shows he cares. He didn't just walk out on me even if I did just pass out drunk on the couch.

I just wish I knew if we did hook up. How can I find out if I don't ask him? We're both still fully clothed, but that doesn't mean anything.

I lean back on the cushion and study him while he sleeps. His long, rough-cut, shaggy blonde hair falls over his face.

I can't see his dark eyes when they're closed, but I know exactly what they look like. I don't have to think too hard to imagine him looking down at me. He always looks down at me with warmth, caring, and kindness.

Red-blonde stubble covers his face and runs down his neck. It makes his neck rough, but that doesn't make his neck any less inviting.

I slept last night with my face buried in that neck. His smell floats into my nostrils even now.

His T-shirt hides his big, beefy body. I can see every inch of the muscles under that shirt going all the way down to his jeans.

What would it be like to touch him right now......to slip my hands under his shirt and run my fingers through the hair on his chest......kiss down his neck and bite his ears to wake him up.....

What would it feel like to hear him growling in my ear when I roll on top of him.....straddle him.....pull up my shirt and bra and shove my breasts in his face and mouth.....feel his hands groping behind my ass to pull me down on top of him.....

My hand sliding between his thighs.....feeling his shaft harden inside his jeans......slipping my hand inside his boxers......his rod throbbing in my hand and his muscles tensing as I stroke him.

My juicy box gliding down on him.....screaming in his ear when he beats into me nice and hard......him flipping me over on the couch and driving into me from behind......him grabbing my hair and spanking against my ass as his gruff, deep voice commands me to respond to him.

Oh, yeah, baby....come on....that's right..... you love it....you feel t hat?.....you like that nice and hard, don't you......come on.....give it to me....give me that ass......Let me hear you scream for me.....yeah, baby, that's so good.....you feel so hot.....

I shut my eyes. I'm starting to get turned on thinking about him. I want to grind on his leg and make him hard right now, but I can't do that.

This is Billy, my friend, my co-worker. He just drove me home from the bar because I was too plastered to drive. He doesn't even think of me that way. He thinks it would be disgusting even to look at me sideways.

I can't keep lying here or I really will start something.

I pry myself off him, sit up, and climb off the couch. He stirs in his sleep.

I go into the kitchen and start making coffee. He rolls onto his side facing away from me.

I find myself studying him from the back. The arch of his rounded muscular shoulder, his unkempt hair, his waist, his legs, his ass.....

What would it be like if he was here as.....what—my boyfriend? My husband? My friend-with-benefits?

I wouldn't want that. I would want more.

Am I really thinking that? Am I really thinking I want more with Billy? Holy shit! My mind staggers at the thought.

I try to distract myself by making coffee, but that only makes the impression stronger that we're a couple. We aren't a couple and we never will be.

He groans, sits up, puts his feet on the floor, and runs his fingers through his hair. His shoulders look powerful and hot from behind. I want to put my arms around him again, but I have to play it off like nothing happened last night.

I take him a cup of coffee and put it in front of him on the coffee table. "Here you go. You like it black, right?"

He mutters, "Thanks," without looking at me.

I can't stand the suspense any longer. "Um.....last night......did we......you know.....do anything?"

"No!" he snaps and his eyes shoot up to meet mine, but only for an instant. He immediately looks away. "Nothing like that."

I wilt in relief. "Oh, phew! I was worried."

He barely glances at me and takes a swig of his coffee. "Thanks for this."

"You said that already. You have today off from work, don't you?"

He nods down at his coffee cup. This is by far the longest we've ever gone without eye contact. Now I know he feels uncomfortable.

Is it because we both crashed in my apartment? Does he think he overstepped?

"I have to go to work," I tell him. "I guess I'll see you at the firehouse barbeque later today."

He nods again. "I guess."

I stare at the side of his face. I want to start something. I want to nuzzle in his ear, nibble his neck, caress him under his shirt—make him feel amazing.

I decide to take the first step, but I make sure not to cross the line.

I rest my head on his shoulder and put my arm behind his back. That's nothing I wouldn't do before. He won't read anything into that.

"Thank you for bringing me home last night," I murmur. "You're my hero even if you don't want to believe it."

He picks up the frame from the floor. "Why did you keep this?"

My head shoots up. "What?"

"Why do you have this? Why did you keep it....and frame it.....and everything? Is it because of me?"

"I....." I stop with my mouth open. What can I say?

I don't even know why I kept that clipping. Sure, I kept it because I like Billy, but not in that way. At least, that's now why I kept it. I guess I just wanted to celebrate his achievement.

He puts the frame on the coffee table and downs the rest of his coffee. "I better go. I'll see you later."

He doesn't wait for me to take my head off his shoulder. Me trying to get close to him must make him uncomfortable.

That clinches it. He would never want anything more with me. He just wants us to be friends the way we always have been.

I can live with that, but it sure would be nice. I can't think of anyone nicer I'd like to go out with. He's hands down the gentlest, most caring, and protective man I've ever met.

The guy just saved my life in a burning building yesterday. What more could I ask?

Chapter 5: Brooke

I push my cart through the grocery store, take a box of cereal off the shelf, and then steer into the produce section. I stop dead in my tracks when I see Billy checking out the bananas.

He glances up and we regard each other across the piles of apples. Is this going to turn into an awkward silence, too? Should I turn around, push my cart to the other side of the store, and avoid him completely?

Without warning, he pulls up two bananas, positions them in his hand to look like guns, and alternately juts them at me while he makes shooting noises with his mouth. "Pow! Pow! You're dead, Brooke."

My hand flies to my chest and I pretend to collapse across my cart. "I'm hit! Call the fire department!"

A few other shoppers nearby stare at us and give us dirty looks. Billy laughs and puts down the bananas. "Too bad these things ran out of ammo."

I straighten up, try not to notice the other shoppers, and steer my cart over to him. This is the first time since that night when we've had a chance to just talk and get back some of our old easy-going ways.

Billy hasn't exactly avoided me. He can't when we work together on almost every shift.

Those questions always hover between us, though, even when we aren't talking about what happened that night.

Nothing happened that night. That's the thing. It only happened in my mind. He isn't even thinking about it.

I do my best to break the ice by not doing anything we wouldn't have done before. "Isn't it a little late for you to be out grocery shopping?" I ask. "It's eight o'clock at night. What's your excuse?"

"I just got off my shift. *You're* out grocery shopping at eight o'clock at night. What's *your* excuse?"

I find myself smirking at him. Billy and I are too good friends to let a little misunderstanding come between us. "I got a craving for bananas." I pick one up and shoot him a crazy grin.

He turns bright red and looks away. "Too much information, sweetheart. Keep that to yourself."

I laugh and put it down. "I don't even like bananas."

"Sacrilege!" he counters. "How can anyone not like bananas? You must be a psychopath."

"You're lucky you didn't wind up in pieces in my basement freezer," I tease.

"Now I know you're lying because you don't have a basement or a freezer." He turns his cart to the carrots and potatoes. "Seriously. What are you doing out of bed? You're going to get in trouble with your mother."

"Only if you tell her."

He grins back at me and we wheel our carts side by side to the meat aisle. He scopes out the freezers. "The price of steak is going up."

"So what else is new? I'll stick with good old-fashioned TV dinners."

"Too much MSG," he counters. "I prefer my food to still be walking and talking."

I explode with laughter. "Now who's the psychopath—and you do have a basement. Remind me never to go anywhere with you alone."

He loads up his cart with a bunch of frozen meats. I load up with TV dinners and a few whole chickens.

"Where are we going after this, Admiral?" I ask.

He puffs out his chest. "Admiral—I like that. Admiral Cates. It sounds kinda like Admiral Kirk, doesn't it?"

I laugh at him. "So what does that make me—Ensign Sulu?"

"You're way better looking than him. Set course for the dairy aisle and....engage."

"Wrong series, genius. That's Captain Jean-Luc Picard, not Captain Kirk."

"Now I know you're a nerd. Who cares who it is? Just go before I set my photon torpedoes to maximum stun."

I turn my cart toward the dairy aisle. He follows me.

We're just turning into the aisle when another shopper comes around the corner. It's a young guy in a business suit. His cart crashes into mine before either of us realizes the other is there.

"Oh! Sorry!" I exclaim and try to pull my cart out of the way.

The guy curls his lip at me. "Get out of the way, you stupid bitch! Didn't you see me coming?"

He slams his cart into mine and tries to push me back so he can get through. I can't move because Billy is right behind me.

Lightning quick, he leaves his cart, sidesteps around me, grabs the front end of the guy's cart, and pushes it aside. "Back off, asshole," Billy snaps. "It was an honest mistake. It was as much your fault as hers. Just go around and go about your business. You don't own the road."

He steers the guy's cart out of the way, but this fool just won't take the hint. "Don't you tell me what to do? Who the hell are you—her boyfriend?"

Billy takes one step toward the guy. "I'm the guy who's gonna kick your ass if you don't back off and go back to what you were doing. You're making a fool of yourself in public. Just steer your cart around her before you get hurt."

The guy checks himself when he sees Billy towering over him. Billy dwarfs the guy by a mile and Billy is twice as broad in the shoulders. The dude's suit just makes him look twerpy by comparison.

The guy's expression changes and he looks away. He steers his cart around mine and disappears into the meat section.

I beam up at Billy. "My knight in shining armor. Thank you."

He shoots the guy a glare from behind. "What an asshole."

I pat his arm. "Never mind. So what strange new life forms are we discovering here, Captain?"

"Admiral," he corrects and makes me laugh again. "Did you know each variety of cheese is colonized by a different species of mold?"

I bend over, stick out my tongue, and pretend to retch on the floor. "I'm never eating cheese again."

"Take a few samples, Mr. Spock. We'll isolate their chemicals for our biological survey."

"You're really taking this Star Trek thing seriously, aren't you?" I take a brick of Monterey Jack off the shelf, add it to my cart, and get a gallon of milk. "So what are you doing for the rest of your evening?"

"I don't have any plans. Do you want to hang out?"

I look up. I didn't expect him to invite me out like that. I thought we were avoiding each other. "Sure. I'd love to," I tell him, "

but no bars and no booze."

"You took the words right out of my mouth. What do you want to do instead? The go-kart race just got brand new cars. We could do that."

"I'm no good at that," I tell him.

"That will make it easier for me to win. Come on. What do you have to lose?"

"Bragging rights?"

He grins at me. "Your lost bragging rights are my gained bragging rights. It's either that or we go bowling and I slaughter you that way."

"Fine. We'll do the go-karts. Just let me take my groceries home first."

"Good. You take your groceries home and meet me back at my place in half an hour."

"Yes, Sir!" I salute him and we both laugh as I push my cart away.

I check out and drive home to put my groceries in the fridge. I don't know about this go-kart business, but I have nothing else to do at eight o'clock on a Saturday night.

Billy and I need to do something to get our friendship back on track. I want to prove we still have a friendship. I need to prove that falling asleep drunk on the couch with him didn't ruin our friendship forever.

What can possibly go wrong driving a go-kart around a track? He'll be in his kart and I'll be in mine. I couldn't come up with a more innocent activity if I tried. It's even more innocent than bowling.

I drive over to his place and find him in his kitchen. His house is much nicer than my apartment.

His house is a sprawling, modern, split-level, four-bedroom house with a big, thriving backyard garden.

Big sliding glass doors lead from the living room to a giant wooden deck overlooking flowering bushes, trees, and even a winding stream and fountain bubbling through the backyard. A picnic table, lounge chairs under an umbrella, and a hot tub sit on the deck.

Billy is the one who built all this. He bought this house when it was rundown and falling apart state, fixed it all up, planted that garden himself, added on the deck, and remodeled most of the house's interior. He's handy that way. He takes pride in his house and he has every right to be.

I'm jealous. I could never do something like this.

Fancy Majorca tile surrounds the kitchen backsplash. No one would ever know the gleaming polished stone countertop is really concrete. Billy ground it to a mirror finish and stained and sealed himself.

The appliances are all retro-chic that he scrouged up from junkyards and garage sales, refurbished, refinished, and restored to beautiful expensive antiques.

This house looks like it's worth millions and he did it all with his own hands. I've been in every room of this house and they're all the same. Every stick of furniture in this house has been lovingly restored to a work of art.

I find him with his head stuck in the fridge. "I'm almost done!" he calls over his shoulder. "I'll be ready to go in a minute."

"Take your time," I tell him. "Did you hear Leila had her baby?"

He shoots me a look over his shoulder. "I was on shift with Keith when he got the call. The dude couldn't scoot out of the firehouse fast enough."

"It's hard to imagine Keith Brewer as a father, isn't it? Can you imagine him cooing and gurgling over his baby?"

"He's the biggest softy there is. He's gonna be great."

"The kid will be driving the firetruck by the time he's three."

Billy laughs. I glance around the living room while I wait for him to finish. A giant leather sectional fills the big, open-plan living room in front of the glass doors leading to the deck.

"Hey, did you get a new coffee table?" I go over to the living room. The lights are off. Moonlight from outside shines on a swooping curve of wood sanded silky smooth. The light plays on every magnificent curve.

"It isn't new," he tells me. "I got the wood off the beach last year. I've been working on the table in my free time. I just finished it."

I kneel down and run my hand over the surface. "It's gorgeous."

"You like it?"

"I love it."

"I spotted it on the beach and knew it was going to be something special. It took me a while to decide how to arrange it."

He shuts the fridge and comes over to me. He bends over and runs his hands over the wood, too.

I get another flashback of what it would be like if he touched me like that—with those big, strong, rough hands.

The shadows surround us here. The light from the kitchen barely makes it this far....and his hand bumps into mine.

He pulls it away. "Oh. Sorry," he mumbles.

I glance up at him...and he glances down at me at the same moment.

Our eyes lock just for a minute. That's the moment when I realize the mind-blowing truth. He has been thinking about me like that. He only felt uncomfortable because he thought I wasn't thinking about him like that.

He stands up immediately and walks back to the kitchen. The moment passes and becomes nothing.

I go back over there and pick up my keys. I guess we're going out to the go-karts now. Oh, well. If he doesn't want it, then it isn't going to happen.

He goes down the hall toward his bedroom. Then he goes into the bathroom, turns on the light, and shuts the door. I hear him in there taking a leak.

He comes out, switches off the bathroom light, and steps forward to reenter the hall on his way back to the living room.

A loud clunk echoes down the hall followed by a crash. "Ow!" he snaps. "Shit! Crap! Damn it!"

I pace down the hall trying to find him. "You okay?"

"Yep." He gasps a few times. "Son of a bitch—that hurt!"

I get as far as the bathroom, but I can't see him in the dark. "Where are you? Do you need a paramedic?"

He starts laughing and then curses again. "Cocksucker!" Then he laughs again. "This isn't funny, Brooke. Don't make light of my suffering."

I chuckle, but just then, I see him stand up right in front of me. He's between me and the bathroom with only a few inches of space between me and the wall.

He has to flatten himself against the wall so he has enough room to stand up. He keeps panting and gasping like he's in pain.

I try to see him in the dark. "Are you sure you're okay?"

"Yeah!" he exclaims. "Just.....I might need a wheelchair."

I laugh....and stop when I realize how close we're standing in the dark hallway. Just enough light comes through the nearby bedroom window for me to see his face. His eyes shine out of the shadows.

I could walk away right now. He'll probably walk away to keep our friendship as platonic as it's ever been.

I don't want it to be platonic. I don't want to walk away and I don't want him to walk away—not until I experience him the way I imagined on my living room couch.

His nostrils flare once as he tries to catch his breath. He's definitely thinking about it, but he holds himself back. He doesn't want to put himself forward in case I don't want him to.

That leaves it up to me to make the first move. I can't hesitate or I'll lose my nerve.

I rest my hand on his chest and feel him stiffen. I let my hand sink a little deeper into him. He's already leaning against the bathroom doorjamb. He can't go anywhere.

My body and mind ignite. I'm about to cross that line....with Billy.

I want that. I want it real bad. I want it more than anything. I want to feel him the way I imagined on the couch.

I lean in and kiss him. His lips respond instantly. I ease my weight down on top of him. His body feels strong and muscular.....and yet soft and safe at the same time.

I rest my whole body against his and kiss him a little deeper. His breath deepens and his lips soften to meet mine. His hands rise to my waist.

I press my lips in a little harder and open my mouth. I want to taste his tongue. The stubble around his lips scratches my face, but that only makes him feel more primal and animalistic. It turns me on.

His mouth starts to open. His tongue darts in once.....and just as fast, he pulls away.

He pushes me off and takes one step down the hall heading back toward the living room. "We shouldn't," he murmurs.

I stand in the same spot watching him. He's right. We shouldn't. We work together at the firehouse. Things would get real awkward if it didn't work out between us—or if one of us got the wrong idea.

"Okay," I whisper back. "We don't have to. It's no big deal. Do you want to go now?"

He nods. I walk past him to go back to the living room, but at the last second, he grabs my arm, spins me back to face him, and attacks me as never before.

He rushes me kissing me fast and hard, pins me against the wall, and crushes me there mauling my mouth and rocking his body into mine.

Chapter 6: Brooke

Billy's breath comes out hot and strained as he leans into me kissing me fast and hard. His prick explodes into a pulsing, rock-hard mass between his legs. Jesus, he must have been dying all this time!

He plants his hands on the wall above his head and arches his muscular chest and stomach down my body to drive his crotch into me. All the explosive desire I felt on the couch comes back with a vengeance.

I gasp as his lips devour mine. I race to keep up with his tongue, his teeth nipping my lips, and then he dives into my neck biting down to my shirt collar.

I pant in rising passion at the sheer power of his desire. He leaves nothing to the imagination, and in a split second, he seizes my shoulders, spins me backward, and shoves me against the wall from behind.

His prick digs into my ass and he drives me hard against the wall. His muscles tense to a wall of iron all the way down to that tight mass between his legs.

He keeps his hands and arms above his head while he spins me out of my mind. This is so much hotter than I ever dreamed it could be. His passion overloads my senses.

He kisses my cheeks, bites my ears, and gnaws down my neck, behind it, and sinks his teeth into my shoulders. He growls at me exactly the way I imagined he would.

That sound sets my hair on end. Is he going to take me right here in the hall?

I want him to. I want him to unleash this monstrous desire on me. I want to take every inch of him and feel all his power consuming me, destroying me, and leaving me weak and breathless.

Without warning, his fingers twine into my hair and he wrenches my head back hard enough to make me yelp.

He keeps mouthing up my cheek, but he can't reach me to kiss me like this. He just holds me arched back like that in primal ecstasy while he hurls his own atomic power at me.

I'm so out of my mind with aching, dripping desire that I don't see him pull my arm behind me. He twists it behind my back and holds me like that to exert his dominance.

Just as fast, just when the overpowering rush of lust and emotion becomes more than I can bear, he moves my hand down to his crotch.

He presses my hand into him and drives his hips into my hand at the same time. I squeeze and he groans as his prick spasms in my hand.

His jeans block me from touching him, but he must want this. He keeps pumping into my hand the more I squeeze and massage him.

"Yes!" he husks. "Yes, baby! Oh, yeah!"

I moan at the sound of that voice—the voice from my fantasies. He's doing it. He's taking me and giving himself to me at the same time.

I want to touch him and for him to ride his body against me at the same time. I don't know what to do next, but in an instant, he pulls away and turns me around again.

He dives in kissing me in greedy mouthfuls and steers me away from the wall without releasing my mouth. I still have to struggle to keep up with his ravenous kisses.

He attacks my clothes, yanks off the jacket and blouse I'm wearing over my T-shirt, and drives me back by the mouth until I stumble into his bedroom.

I've been in here before, but never for anything other than just to hang out with him. It never once crossed my mind that I would come in here for anything like this.

He grabs my jeans trying to unbutton them, leaves that, plunges his hand between my legs, and squeezes me hard through my jeans. I squeal as a lightning bolt of pleasure and aching need spikes through me. I want him. I want him to do so much more than this.

We bump into the bed, but he doesn't stop. He pushes me down so I flop on the bedspread.

He climbs on top of me still kissing me and shoving his tongue down my throat. His hands claw and grasp and grope all over me.

He's escalating faster than I can keep up with him, but he doesn't try to take it any further than this. He definitely doesn't try to undress me any more than I already am.

He straddles my hips with his knees outside them. He can't get to me like this. Why won't he go any further?

He stretches his arms and hands above our heads again. He doesn't bring his hands down except to stroke my hair while we kiss.

My eyes float open and my breath catches when I see him staring into me with those deep dark eyes. I can't read anything in them but volcanic desire barely holding back.

That look brings back all my hidden longing from that morning on the couch. He won't touch me more than this.

We've already crossed the line. We're kissing and he's rubbing against my body with his prick as hard as a rock. We're going there, but he won't take the next step—not by himself.

I slip my hands under his T-shirt and feel his muscles straining to the breaking point. He rocks into me with every caress of my hands. My touch obviously turns him on beyond belief.

It turns me on beyond belief, too. I trail my fingers through the hair on his chest and feel his nipples underneath. Every part of him feels magnificent, powerful, and yet soft and welcoming. I crave every part of him.

He keeps drilling his iron spike into me from above, but he doesn't try to spread my legs. I want more.

I creep a little lower trying to touch him. He lifts off me enough to let me squeeze him through his jeans, but I want the real thing.

I find his waistband. All this grinding drives his jeans down far enough for me to feel the rough hair at the bottom of his stomach, but as soon as I try to unbutton his jeans, he changes position again.

He straightens up on his hands and knees, flips me onto my stomach, and lowers his weight onto me from above. He keeps his knees outside my thighs and even uses his legs to compress mine together.

He drills into my ass the way he did in the hall, but this feels different. I'm lying face down on his bed like his.....I don't know what to call myself. A thousand dirty words rush into my mind. *Animal. Whore. Bitch. Toy.*

My desire turns dark. I want to be dirty. I want him to make me feel every shade of passion in my soul, even the dark ones—especially the dark ones. I want him to unleash that part of me.

He would never call me any of those names. He respects me too much. He held himself back because he didn't want to betray that respect.

Now it all breaks through the surface and I want it. He grabs my arms and pulls them above my head. He doesn't pin me by anything other than his weight grinding into me from behind.

That extra little bit of extension explodes me out of my senses. I moan in ecstasy and arch my ass into his thrusts.

"You like that, huh?" he snarls in my ear. "You want that hard prick in your ass, baby? You love that, don't you? Come on. Show me how much you want it."

That voice speaks to me out of my darkest fantasies. I rear back trying to shove my ass into his thrusts. I want him to take me all the way. I want him to strip me, use me, drill me, pulverize me.

He stretches his legs out parallel with mine. His weight falls more heavily across my back.

Before I know what he plans to do, he seizes my hair in one hand, rips my head back, and jams his other hand down my jeans into my panties.

His fingers plunge into me and his hot breath sears my ear as he hisses through clenched teeth. "Beg for it, baby," he snarls. "Beg for me to take you. Let me hear you scream for it. Come on. That's right. You are so fucking hot. You know you need this."

I scream out and don't even try to be quiet as his fingers blast me apart. I need this. God damn, I need this! I try to drive down on those fingers, but Billy does it for me.

He drills his prick into my ass to drive me down on his own fingers. He crushes my body between his iron chest and his fingers plunging to my deepest core.

I scream louder—as loud as I can. All my torrential desire pours out of me and hot juice gushes around his fingers.

I hear him bellowing in my ear, but I can't hear him over my own screams. His fingers tighten in my hair. His breath stings my ear and neck as he yells commands for me to disintegrate in his hands.

This is beyond anything I imagined. He's taking me out of my mind to some other place. I don't recognize myself and this primal beast I'm becoming.

I rupture into a world-destroying orgasm beyond anything I ever thought possible. My body convulses in his hand and tremors lightning between my legs to spread to the rest of my body.

I spasm back and forth between pushing my ass into his thrusts and forcing myself down on his fingers. He holds me so tightly that I can only buck against his hand to take his fingers deeper.

I can't stop screaming on and on and on. Will it ever end?

Chapter 7: Brooke

Somewhere in all my dizzy, drunken rapture, Billy eases off me. He's just as hard as ever, but he stops pounding into me from behind. He draws his saturated fingers out of my panties and leaves me sobbing and whining on the bedspread while he rolls off onto the bed next to me.

I can only stare in front of me still moaning as the last shudders die. He puts his fingers in his mouth to suck them clean. I can't look. I buckle onto the bed and bury my face in the bedspread.

I'm still fully dressed. He didn't even do it with me, but he still gave me the greatest ecstasy I've ever experienced. I never thought it could be like that.

He leans in close without trying to turn me over. He strokes my hair like he might be trying to clear it away from my face, but he doesn't succeed completely.

I feel him kissing my hair and the side of my face, but I can't look up. I can't move at all. My body feels wrung out.

I keep my face buried in the bedspread moaning and whimpering. I can't stop shaking. I feel like I'm having a million tiny orgasms one after another as ripples of energy pulse through me.

He leans a little closer. His body radiates heat into me from the side, but he doesn't roll on top of me. He just lies there next to me. He's here. He didn't just walk away and leave me after that.

He lies there for a second. He doesn't try to take it any further. Does he want to?

I know he does. His prick must be aching from the pressure, but he doesn't even try to do anything. He doesn't mention taking care of himself.

He tries one more time to rake the hair out of my eyes. "Kiss me, baby," he whispers. "Kiss me."

He pushes my head back just enough to bring my lips into the open. He burrows against my raised arms and finally locks his lips with mine.

I kiss him, but he kisses gently now. His tongue slides into my mouth and floods me with warmth. He doesn't try to escalate any farther than that. Is he really satisfied with what we just did?

Kissing him brings all my desires back to the surface. Maybe they never really left.

I raise my head a little higher....and then I know I want more. He might be satisfied with this, but I'm not. We've come this far. I want it all.

I climb onto my hands and knees and kiss him more deeply. His eyes gleam up at me from below, but he questions me with those eyes. He doesn't know what I want or how badly I want it. I'll just have to show h im.

Now I'm the one to use my mouth to push him down onto his back. He relaxes under me on the bed, but this isn't what I want.

I rip open my jeans and kick them off while we're still kissing. I grab his hand and steer it between my legs again. I want that. I want it all.

He slides his already wet fingers in and I explode all over again. I slam down on his fingers and he pumps them into me just as hard.

That could never be enough. I climb on top of him devouring his mouth, snaking my tongue around his, and stroking his face, hair, neck, and body as fast as I can.

His fingers between my legs drive me wild and I let the beast off its chain. I straddle his hips and grind on his hard prick. His deep groan of desire skyrockets me out of my mind.

I tear off his lips, pull up his T-shirt, and maul his chest with my hungry mouth. "Baby...." he gasps. "Oh, God, baby....."

I want that sound in my ears always. I want to feel him shivering when I drag my lips across his nipples and bite down his stomach.

I shove his shirt up until he tears it off over his head with one hand. He doesn't take the other one out from between my legs. I'm plunging myself onto his fingers too hard and rising too fast to stop.

I strip up my shirt and bra and shove my breasts into his face. He responds immediately, flattens his other hand against my back, and attacks my breasts sucking, biting, nipping, and licking.

I scream again, and just as fast, I blast into orbit in another reeling climax more powerful than the first. I grind down and squash his hand against his own prick. His fingers electrify me. I can't stop screaming, thrusting, and bucking against his hand.

He bites my nipples hard. My breasts suffocate him, but he doesn't stop or slow down at all.

I'm still screaming from all this torrential energy pouring through me when he shoves his hand between my legs—his other hand, but he doesn't touch me. He doesn't take his fingers out of me.

He strips open his jeans, bucks his hips into the air to scoot them down, and kicks them off.

He pulls his dripping fingers out of my sodden, quivering channel. I swim out of my delirium enough to see his straining veiny shaft pointing up at me.

"Come on, baby," he whispers. "Come on."

This is what I want. This is what I dreamed about. What is this all leading to if not the real deal?

He clasps hold of my hips and guides me down. I have to readjust my position to straddle him, but before I can get there, he rears off the bed, straps his arm around me, and turns me over onto my back.

He kneels between my spread thighs now. He's naked with his rock-hard shaft pointed straight at me, but he doesn't dive right in.

He tugs my shirt off and unclips my bra to remove it completely. He exposes every part of me. Even then, he leaves me lying naked on his bed where he can see me.

He leans in on his hands and knees and kisses me. He's still kissing me and gazing into my eyes when he slowly, carefully, gently, deliberately eases between my legs and drills inside.

I gasp and my eyes clamp shut at the intensity of his thickness. He cracks me open and that feeling spikes me off the charts again. I scream into his mouth. I can't stop it.

He breaks off and pushes up on his arms. He looks so much bigger like this.

He corkscrews his hips in wicked spiral thrusts to impale me all the way to my limit. I clamp my eyes shut and scream every time he drives in.

As soon as he locks his bones against mine, he draws back and my eyes pop wide open to stare at him.

That ice-hot feeling of his shaft gliding out of me on a river of wetness—it electrifies me as much as anything. I lie sprawled on his bed with my arms above my head.

I see myself exposed. He can watch my breasts swaying to his rhythm, my thighs spread for him—my whole body surrendered to whatever he wants to do to me.

He doesn't want to do anything except take me to the stars. I know that now—as if I could ever think anything else about him.

He takes his time before he picks up his pace. His eyes keep questioning me the whole time. Do I want this? Do I want him? Do I enjoy what he's doing?

Can't he see from the dreamy ecstasy written all over my face that I'm in Heaven? Can't he see my body trembling for him and the spasmodic waves of convulsive rapture rocketing through me every time he fills me full of his throbbing hot flesh?

His muscles strain as he increases his rhythm. His thighs slap against mine as he drives me up with each thrust. My breasts bounce in front of his eyes. God, yes, I need this! I need every inch of him.

He grabs one of my legs under the knee and pushes it up in a full stretch. That extra space gives him the room to pound in even harder. I scream as the next spike of orgasm tears me apart.

He attacks with all the fury and animal madness he showed me out in the hall. He leans forward and hooks my knee over his shoulder.

His drilling power blows me out of this world. He glares down at me and those eyes leave me nowhere to hide.

I arch into each brutal thrust as spike after spike of catastrophic intensity sweeps me out of my mind.

He follows my movement and uses the same leg to rotate me onto my stomach. He pushes that leg up and slams into me from behind.

This is my dream coming true—the dream that he would flood me with himself and take over all control. I can't stand the sheer overwhelming pleasure he's giving me.

I can scream all I want now, but I can't bury my face in the bed to hide from him.

He arches over me and his husky breath in my ear tells me he's cycling up to that crescendo of fulfilment just as fast as I am.

His cruel thrusts catapult me over the edge. I can't stop screaming and crying and keening as I tumble into a vast sea of bliss. He collapses over me as his body still arches to the same unified rhythm.

Chapter 8: Billy

I wake up again with Brooke's head on my chest and her arms around me, but this is nothing like last time.

We lie totally naked on my bed. We're in my bedroom....and we're naked.

I could never, ever forget what we did in here—not if I live a thousand years. Never have I experienced anything like that.

I stare at the ceiling and try not to breathe. I don't want to break the spell.

The sun is just coming up outside. We've been here all night. God only knows when we stopped doing it, but it couldn't have been that long before sunrise.

We've been lying here ever since. I don't want to do anything to shatter the illusion that we might stay like this forever.

I don't know if she's asleep. She doesn't move any more than I do. If she's asleep, I don't want her to wake up. I don't want her to start regretting last night.

I'll never regret it. Not ever.

She's every bit as sweet as I dreamed she would be—even more so because she's real. Every handful of her glorious body feels impossibly good. Every taste of her delicious flesh makes me crave her more.

I can't believe I got lucky enough to spend one night with her. I'm not so stupid that I would expect ever to repeat it in my life. I'm not that lucky.

She feels incredible lying here next to me. The heat from her succulent breasts radiates into my side. Her slippery juice still stains her thighs where her leg hangs over my knee. My God, what a goddess this is lying in my arms right now!

She doesn't even know how beautiful and special she is. She has no idea how much I want to ravage her all over again—not just for one night, but forever.

That will never happen. We stayed up all night in the throes of passion. Now we both have to get up and go to work.

We're working together today. That's gonna get real interesting.

Things will start to look different in the light of day. They always do.

How would it even work— both of us working at the firehouse?

Keith and Leila have always worked together, but I'm not Keith Brewer. Danny and Emily just started working together and now Josh and his new wife Chris are doing it.

None of them is me. Brooke might be able to pull that off, but not me.

The sky gets lighter outside. We can't lie here forever, but I still don't dare even to check the time. I would rather show up late for work than lose this moment.

Her soft voice drifts into my ear. "Are you awake?"

I barely manage to croak, "Yes. Are you?"

She laughs. Her body shakes against me. She feels so delicious like that. I wind up smirking even though she can't see me.

She pushes herself up on her elbow....and the look in her smoking hot face gives me butterflies.

Her hair spills over her face all glowing with sex. I've never seen her like this.

She looks absolutely angelic. Her eyes glisten with pleasure....and something else. Some emotion beams out at me when she gazes down at me.

I want to kiss her. I want to run my fingers through her hair and tell her.....everything. I never want to let her out of my bed.

She leans in and kisses me before I think to stop her. Why would I want to stop her?

My heart cracks when she kisses me so softly.

This is nothing like last night. She was an animal last night and she let me take her like that.

She loved it. She screamed for it. She came for me again and again in ways I'll dream about for the rest of my life.

Now she kisses me in velvet softness—and all that emotion comes through her lips. Is she trying to tell me something?

I don't dare to believe that. She'll get up and go on with her life the way she always does. She doesn't need me dragging her down.

She leans back and cracks another grin. That smile lights me up, but it also tells me plain as day that this won't last. Nothing this good can last.

"I don't suppose you have a uniform that will fit me that I can borrow for work today, do you?" she asks.

I snort. "Not unless you want to go as Bozo the Clown."

"Hey, it beats you trying to wear one of my uniforms, right?"

Now it's my turn to laugh, but before I can answer, she rotates on top of me. Her naked body touches me all the way down to my crotch.

She kisses me deeply, passionately, deliciously. She sways her body on top of me and undulates her sweet, juicy box down on my package.

I start to get hard. She is not going to start up again—not when we both have to go to work.

I don't dare to stop her. I squeeze her hips and ass, slide my hands up her back, cradle the back of her neck while we kiss, and follow her slow, aching rotations that drive me out of my mind.

I want to slide into her and make her spasm with a million orgasms again, but right then, an alarm goes off on her phone. She must have left it in her jacket pocket. Her jacket lies right outside my room on the hall floor.

She groans and rakes her hair out of her face while she glances over at it. "Damn that reality. I'm going to speak to the manager and get it banned."

"Let me know when you get the policy changed so I can start skipping reality, too."

She climbs off me to go turn off her alarm. That's the signal. Last night is officially over.

I sit up. Now, being naked around her feels like the most inappropriate thing I could possibly be.

I grab a pair of pajama pants from the bedside table drawer and slip them on while her back is turned.

She kneels down on the floor, pulls her phone out of her jacket, taps it to turn off the alarm, and then stares at the screen reading something.

She glances up at me and her expression changes when she sees me in my pajama pants. Her eyes dart around the room.

I can just see the wheels turning in her head. We did it. We did more than it. I don't know what to call last night, but it was more than just doing it.

I don't broach the subject and neither does she, but I can see the cogs grinding in that brain of hers.

What is she thinking? What is she feeling? What conclusions is she coming to about....us?

She finally asks, "Do you mind if I take a shower?"

"Sure," I tell her. "There are towels in the bathroom closet."

She nods. She already knows her way around my house.

She darts around the room grabbing her clothes as fast as she can. I try not to look at her naked body, now that the moment has passed.

I slump as soon as the bathroom door closes behind her. I prop my elbows on my knees and pass my hand across my eyes. What the hell did I just do?

I may have just ended one of the greatest friendships of my life. God knows I need all the friends I can get.

She's always been there for me, always supported me, always backed me up. She's probably the person I've been the closest to on the whole fire crew.

Now that's over. Jesus Christ! I must not deserve a friend like her if I could throw it all away like this.

I still have to go to work today. I have to pay the bills—which means I have to work with her. The thought makes me cringe.

I go out to the kitchen and start making breakfast. That's the least I can do for her.

I make coffee, fry bacon and scrambled eggs, and make toast. I put her breakfast on the table for her, eat my own, and then start getting my uniform and other gear ready for my shift.

I straighten out the bed to erase all evidence of everything we did. I clean up my room and put yesterday's uniform in the laundry.

No one would ever know what we did in this room, but I know. Those memories, those sounds and sensations—they'll remain etched into my flesh for all time. I'll never get rid of them.

She comes out of the bathroom fully dressed with her hair wet. She takes one look at me walking around shirtless in my pajama pants and immediately looks away. She must not like what she sees. Of course not. Everything looks different in daylight.

"Your breakfast is on the table," I tell her. "You probably need to go home and get your uniform before you go to work."

She nods, sits down at the table, and takes a drink of her coffee. "Thank you for this."

"I'm gonna get in the shower, so I probably won't see you before you go home. I'll see you at the firehouse, okay?"

"Okay." She looks up at me and her eyes lock on me.

Her lips tremble like she wants to say something. What is she about to say?

Is she going to say something about last night? Is she going to tell me just to forget it and pretend like it never happened?

I'm cool with that if that's what she wants. I know better than to expect anything else.

She doesn't say anything. "You okay?" I ask.

"Yeah. Thank you for the breakfast. I'll see you at the firehouse."

"Okay. Have a good day."

I bolt and barricade myself in the bathroom. She's gone by the time I come out.

Chapter 9: Billy

I get to the firehouse as fast as I can and make it just in time to clock in. Brooke shows up a few minutes later.

Everyone is so busy starting the shift that they don't notice her coming late. We're both assigned to the rescue truck again, but she's working with Sophie McNish.

They work on the paramedics' drug box and other stuff. I work with the guys checking out the rest of the truck. No one notices Brooke and me avoiding each other.

Are we avoiding each other? I sure hope working with her isn't going to be like this from now on. That would be a nightmare, especially if anyone found out why.

What if John finds out Brooke and I hooked up? I cringe. This could lead to me losing the best job I've ever had—not to mention people I care about who are actually starting to respect me.

I can't let that happen, but I already did let it happen because I already let hooking up with her happen.

I shouldn't have done that. That's why I keep her as a friend. I should have remembered that.

I doubt I could have hooked up with her before. I mean, I never would have believed I could.

Even if I knew she wanted to, I probably wouldn't have. I wouldn't want anything to spoil our friendship or the job.

That must not be true because I let it happen anyway. I really am a loser.

I find myself casting sidelong glances in her direction as the shift wears on. She looks as amazing today as she always does. Now I'm the asshole I need to protect her from and I couldn't even do that.

I still want her. That's what really breaks me up. I still want her in my bed like that—and not just in my bed. I want her in my arms....kissing me....showering in my bathroom....I don't want to lose that, but I never really even had her.

I try to tell myself not to look, but I wind up looking anyway. I can't help it.

I really screwed up, but I can't even tell anyone or do anything to fix it. I just have to wait for it to blow up in my face the way I know it will.

Everybody goes upstairs to the break room after we finish all our morning chores. The rest of the crew fires jokes back and forth as usual.

"Is it true some jackass from the building downtown actually had the nerve to file a complaint against you and Brooke for taking too long to get the employees out of the building?" Sophie asks me.

"It wasn't the guy with pen ink on his shirt, was it?" Ellis asks.

"He wasn't in the building, dumbass," Keith growls at him. "She's talking about someone Brooke and Billy brought down in the crane bucket."

"He could have come down real quick if he just jumped from the window," Caleb points out. "Then he wouldn't have to ride in the bucket."

"It's only one guy," I tell him. "The other employees are all vouching for us."

"Still, you gotta admire the balls on a guy who complains about firefighters saving his damn life," Ellis goes on.

"We don't have to admire him for anything," Danny chimes in. "He's an ungrateful bastard. You and Brooke should have left him in the building."

"We couldn't do that," Brooke replies. "Besides, we didn't know he would complain until after we already got him down."

She and Sophie sit down on the couch. Sophie sits in the middle and Brooke sits on one end.

I'm just taking a bottle of juice out of the fridge when Sophie notices me. "Do you want to sit next to Brooke? Here you go."

She scoots down to the end of the couch to leave the spot next to Brooke open for me to sit down. Brooke doesn't even look at me.

"That's okay," I tell Sophie. "I gotta go downstairs and get something out of my locker anyway."

I walk out of the breakroom. I don't see if anyone noticed me trying to avoid Brooke.

How long we will have to avoid each other before someone notices or at least stops expecting us to joke around with each other the way we used to?

Now I have no choice but to go downstairs, open my locker, and pretend to take something out of it.

I groan, sigh, and pass my hand across my eyes. This is turning into the worst day ever.

I'm just making up my mind to hide in the locker room for the rest of eternity when the fire alarm goes off.

Everyone tumbles down the stairs real quick. I get to the truck first and hop in the front, so at least I don't have to see Brooke getting into her turnouts. That is the last thing I need right now.

Keith gets into the driver's seat a second later. "Any news coming in from dispatch?"

I check the computer. That gives me a perfect excuse not to look in the back. I hear Brooke and Sophie talking back there.

Danny, Caleb, and Ellis talk, too, but for some reason, Brooke's voice carries more than the others. Everything she does sticks out so I can't ignore it.

"Car accident on the highway," I read. "Four cars involved. No word yet on any injuries."

"Let's go save the day." Keith puts the truck in gear and we pull out onto the road. Josh and Chris follow in one ambulance. Andy Skinner and Naomi McFee follow in the second ambulance.

The Police direct us into position and Keith divides us up between the four cars. "One paramedic per car. Brooke and Billy, check that one over there. Josh, you and Caleb take that car. Naomi, you come with me and Chris...."

"You forgot about me," Andy chimes in.

Keith pretends not to hear. "Chris, you go with Ellis and see about that pickup over there." Keith finally can't ignore Andy anymore. The guy might be a useless prick, but he's still part of the crew. "Andy, you man the ambulance and triage any walking wounded we send over to you."

Andy starts to pout like he usually does, but we all know he isn't any good for real work.

The rest of us split up to our assignments. Of course Keith had to assign me to work with Brooke. We always work together.

That's never been a problem before now. No one knows about last night and they never will if I have anything to say about it.

I just have to buckle down and keep it professional. We're on a call here. This isn't the high school basketball court and she isn't some teenager, either. We're both professional emergency personnel.

She gets her game face on right away, so she must be thinking the same thing. "You wanna take the passenger?" she murmurs to me on our way to the car. "I'll take the driver."

"Check it out," I tell her. "They got two car seats in the back."

"I see. Let's go."

I circle the car on the passenger side The driver is a young woman with messed up blonde curls. The passenger is a young man about the same age.

The two kids in the back can't be more than two and three. They both sit in their car seats bawling their heads off, but they look fine.

I don't see any injuries on the woman, either, but the man doesn't look good. His chin hangs on his chest.

His face is a mass of smashed, bloody pulp. A bloody shattered circle of broken glass marks the windshield where his face hit the glass.

Blood oozes from under his shirt where his chest hit the dashboard.

The woman leans across the seat yelling in the guy's ear. "Michael!! Michael!!"

Her reaction scares the kids more than anything, but I don't have time to do anything about that. I put the jump kit down on the ground, stick my head, arms, and shoulders through the passenger window, and close my hands around the guy's head on either side.

I pry his head up and hold him there with his spine braced. That's the best I can do until Brooke comes to help me.

She sticks her head, arms, and shoulders through the driver's window and yells over the woman's screams. "Ma'am! Ma'am—look at me!"

The woman doesn't hear her. "Michael!!" the woman screeches. "MICHAEL!!"

"MA'AM!!" Brooke roars and actually grabs the woman to make her turn around. "Is that your husband? We're going to take care of him, but you need to get out of the vehicle. DO YOU HEAR ME?!! Get out of the vehicle, get your children, and take them to that ambulance over there! MA'AM!! We can't help him with you and the children in the car. Understand?!"

The woman finally wakes up enough to hear what Brooke is saying. I'm glad Brooke is here to yell in the woman's face like that. I couldn't do it without losing my cool entirely.

Brooke pulls out of the car, opens the door, and steers the woman to get out. Then Brooke helps unbuckle the two kids.

She shoots me a look on the side. "You okay for now?"

I nod. We're both in emergency mode. All our awkwardness vanishes instantly.

Brooke gets the first kid out. He's the older one and he shrieks even more when she picks him up. He bursts out crying when she puts him in his mother's arms.

She starts to walk away before Brooke gets the little girl unbuckled. Fortunately, Sophie shows up a minute later and takes the little girl off Brooke's hands.

Brooke gets back into the rear seat behind the man. "Okay!" she pants. "I'm gonna take his head from you. Then you come back here and take his head again. You'll be able to hold him better from here so we can immobilize him. Okay?"

I nod. I don't question anything she says. I just have to follow her orders.

She winds up touching my hands when she places her hands around the patient's head to support his spine. I try not to notice her touching me, but this is just work. It doesn't mean anything.

It starts to mean something when I crawl into the back seat next to her. We have to cram in with our bodies right next to each other.

I have to put my arms in front of and through hers to get back in position behind the patient. I practically have to sit on her lap and then I close my hands over hers to take the patient's head.

I catch her glancing at me at the same time I glance at her. Her eyes look the same way they did this morning.....when she was lying on top of me stark naked on my bed.....when she was kissing me and rubbing her satin body all over me.....

I push those thoughts away and concentrate on the job at hand. She pulls her hands out from under mine and then wriggles out of the back seat. Now I'm all alone back here.

She isn't here anymore, but I still struggle to deal with all these feelings rushing through me. Will it be like this for the rest of forever—every time I have to work with her—every time I even look into her eyes?

She gets out of the car and goes back to working on the patient from the driver's seat. Chris, Ellis, Josh, and Keith show up a minute later and they all start working to extricate the patient.

Brooke gives all of them orders. She gives me orders, too. "Get in through the driver's door, Ellis. Hold his head from the front so Billy can move his hands out of the way. Do you got him, Billy?"

"I got him," I reply in as neutral a voice as possible.

She's working a mile a minute to check the patient's pupils, put him on oxygen, and suction his nose and mouth at the same time Ellis and I get a cervical collar around the patient's neck.

Then I have to hold the guy for another eternity while Keith, Danny, Ellis, and Caleb get the backboard ready to take the guy out of the car.

"You're gonna pass his head back to Danny, Billy," Brooke yells at me over dozens of other voices all talking and negotiating at the same time. "Ready?"

"Ready," I tell her.

I hand off to Danny and then the four of them swivel the guy onto the backboard. I'm done for now.

I climb out of the car just as they're putting the patient on a gurney. Brooke is still working on him as fast as she can.

She goes with him to the ambulance and loads up to drive him to the hospital. Chris and Josh both go with her and Caleb drives them. Everyone else is still working.

The wind goes out of my sails, now that Brooke is gone. Working with her is still the bright spot in my shift even if things are awkward and strained between us.

They won't always be. Things will go back to normal. I know that now.

We'll always be able to work together. We're both too committed to the job.

John comes over to me. "You okay?" he asks.

I nod. "I'm fine."

I turn away and go back to helping the rest of the crew. They're all boarding up their patients and triaging the ones who can still walk. That gives me plenty of lifting, carrying, and strapping down to do.

Then we just secure the scene and it's time to head back to the firehouse.

"Any word on Brooke and the others?" I ask Keith when we get into the truck.

I try to keep my tone casual, but he's too used to me asking about Brooke to notice anything unusual. "They just cleared the hospital. They're on the way back to the firehouse now."

I get a pang of uncertainty. I can't decide if I want to see Brooke at the firehouse or not. Am I actually dreading seeing her? How did it come to this?

Chapter 10: Brooke

I walk into the firehouse locker room at the end of my shift. Billy walks out of it the minute I show my face.

He's been avoiding me all day. He couldn't avoid me on that car accident call-out, but that only makes it more obvious. This strain between us will keep causing us problems.

He didn't say anything at his house about us hooking up. I didn't say anything, either, but I don't know what to say. What can I say—that he gave me the greatest night of sex I've ever had in my life?

What if he just wants it to be a one-night fling and nothing else? What if he just wants to go back to being friends?

I couldn't tell him all the other things I've been thinking about him—about making him coffee in the morning and him cooking me breakfast and waking up in each other's arms and all that.

I don't even know how I feel about all that and it hasn't even happened. It never will happen because we're friends. Last night was a colossal mistake—nothing else.

I can't stand this tension hanging in the air between us. I have to at least broach the subject. Billy will never do it.

I leave my stuff in my locker and race outside to the parking lot. Our shift went longer than usual. It's dark outside and Billy is just getting into his truck.

I rush up on the passenger side and call through the open window. "Hey! Don't leave. We need to talk."

He doesn't stop putting his key in the ignition. "What do you want to talk about?"

"You know what I want to talk about. We need to talk about last night."

I throw caution to the wind, pull open the door, and climb into the passenger seat. We are NOT talking about this through his truck window. That would be beyond tacky.

I shut the door behind me and the dome light switches off. The streetlamps around the firehouse parking lot give plenty of light for us to see each other.

He stiffens for a second and then shrugs. "Okay. What do you want to talk about?"

"We have to talk about what happened between us. We have to decide what it means—or if it means anything."

"Why does it have to mean anything? It happened. What more is there to say?"

"Nothing. It's just...." I hesitate. What exactly do we need to say about it besides that it happened? "I don't want this to ruin our professional relationship."

"Neither do I," he replies. "Everything worked out fine on that call, didn't it?"

"Yeah, but...." I gulp. He really isn't making this any easier. "I don't want it to ruin our friendship, either."

He softens instantly and changes his tone. He lowers his voice to a murmur—a low, broken murmur.

That voice reminds me so much of last night. "I don't want that either, sweetheart. That's why we should just let it go. It happened. It doesn't have to ruin anything."

I want to say more. I want....more.

I don't want to let it go. I want him, but I can't tell him that.

Saying I don't want it to ruin our friendship makes it sound like I *don't* want more. Saying that makes it sound like I don't want to think about it ever again.

I throw back my shoulders. I have to do this. "Our friendship is the most important thing. Let's agree not to let it happen again."

He nods. "Absolutely. We both slipped up. We can correct and get the train back on the tracks. Nothing has to change."

I nod, too. I can't help myself. "Right."

He waits for me to say something else. "You okay? Was there anything else?"

I look up at him. The light coming through the windows reflects off his cheekbones, his shaggy hair...and the rest of him.

His truck cab isn't as dark as the hall outside his bathroom, but the shadows give the same impression. We're sitting here alone in the dark in the middle of the night.

I get a sudden charge of desire for him. I've been fantasizing about him all day. Does he feel the same way about me?

I open my mouth to say something—like what? That I want to do it with him after all?

Get out of the truck, Brooke. Get out of the truck right now.

His magnetic power draws me in. I can't tear my eyes away from him.

Now I know exactly what touching him feels like. I know exactly what he looks and feels like under his clothes.

Thinking that sends a rush of heat between my legs. My tissues swell and a slippery film of ooze dampens my panties. Neither of us got any sleep last night, but thinking about it only makes me want him more.

I more than want him. I crave him. I'm obsessed with him. I can't stop thinking about him.....the way he took me....the way he crushed me under his weight.....the way he clenched his fingers in my hair....

He peers at me in the dim light. "Is everything all right?" he asks in the same soft undertone. "Do you need something?"

I can't bring myself to speak, but I already know what I'm going to do this.

I lay my hand on his leg.....right above the knee.

He stiffens again and his eyes harden into a glare.... exactly the way he looked at me last night.

I inch my fingers a little higher up his thigh....and squeeze. His whole body tenses. I feel his muscles strain and his chest tightens.

"I need this....Billy....." I half-whisper. "I need.....you."

He scowls at me even more darkly, but the rush of heat bulging under his uniform pants tells me he wants it, too.

I take a chance, let my hand migrate just a little higher, and squeeze right in the crease between his high and his package.

My other hand drifts to his chest......and under his T-shirt to his skin and hair.

"I need......you.....Billy.....like this......" I let my right hand stroke across his strained bulge. He throbs under my touch.

I massage a little harder......and let my hand circle his whole package to grip his balls, too.

He groans and shuts his eyes as his head falls back against the seat headrest. "Christ, baby!" he husks. "What are you doing to me?"

I can't stop touching him. "I need this......" I whisper. "I need you so bad....."

He doesn't open his eyes. His tortured breath rasps between bared, gritted teeth. He spasms under my hand when I stroke him in a steady rhythm.

Without warning, he raises his hand, closes it on my breast through my T-shirt, and squeezes in a matching rhythmic crush.

I gasp out a broken moan of pure, unbridled lust. My body spasms and swells with painful desire between my legs.

"Billy....!" I whimper.

He groans again in an animal snarl of primal hunger and ravenous desire. He doesn't stop me from squeezing and stroking him through his pants. He feels so strong and thick and mean in there. I want him more than anything.

The feeling of his hand compressing my breast sends wave upon wave of blistering passion through me. I can't stop moaning and whining as the energy builds.

I want to climb on top of him, but I can't do that when he's sitting behind the wheel of his truck. I mean, I could, but doing it right here in the firehouse parking lot seems so cheap.

I would do it if it meant climbing on his lap and sitting down on him. I would do a lot more than that to feel him inside me and his hands taking control of me.

His breath catches again and his dark eyes float open to meet mine. His hard gaze holds me spellbound as he moves his hand down between my legs.

He grips me there, squeezing, massaging, turning me on beyond my wildest desires.

I can't stop moaning as I ride down on his powerful hand. He knows exactly how to turn me on.

I keep rubbing his shaft through his pants. His chest feels etched in power under his T-shirt.

I don't know how to contain all this energy building up in me. I'm going to explode right now.

I can't hold back when he leans across the seat, buries his rough face in the side of my neck, and bites. His teeth and hot breath crawl up to my ear and send a prickle over my scalp.

That sensation merges with all the moist heat pulsing between my legs right now. His other hand clamps on my breast while he still drives me to the breaking point between my legs.

I feel myself careening over the edge of some vast precipice. I'll never come back from this, but he's holding me and carrying me there so fast I can't stop.

His fingers clench in my hair and he pulls my head back so he can maul my neck in cruel bites. That pushes me over the edge and I scream out as the first wave detonates me in climax.

Before I can scream loudly enough for everyone in the damn firehouse to hear me, he steers my mouth to his and kisses me to stifle the sound.

He doesn't stop rubbing me to a blistering climax. He holds me there roaring and sobbing into his mouth while he destroys every last shred of my reserve.

He reduces me to a whimpering, quivering mass in his arms and finally lets my head fall on his shoulder.

I lie there twitching and moaning, but he doesn't let me go. He pets my hair, kisses the side of my face, and strokes his big, warm hands up and down my back and arms and the back of my neck.

I can't cope with this. I want Billy so bad, but we just decided to stay friends. I don't know what this means.

I don't know what it means that he's holding me like this, either. Does he want more? Is that why he's being so gentle and caring?

After what seems like hours, he closes both hands around my cheeks and raises my head. I can't do it myself. He kisses me for a minute and then leans back.

When I open my eyes, I see that he's still as hard as a rock. He doesn't try to push me to do more. He doesn't mention taking care of himself nor does he ask me to do anything for him.

He pushes me back and straightens me out in the passenger seat before he sits up. "Buckle up," he tells me.

I don't know what he means until he turns the ignition and starts pulling out of the parking lot.

My heart turns another somersault. I guess we're leaving together. I don't ask where we're going.

Chapter 11: Billy

I can barely breathe when I park my truck in front of my house with Brooke in the passenger seat. I don't know what's about to happen except that we're here together.

We just made out in my truck after deciding we wouldn't. It sure looks like we're about to do it again. How should I feel about that?

I should stop it. I should insist that we keep this platonic, but the time to do that was before she started touching me.

Once she did, it was all downhill from there. Her hands on me drive everything else out of my mind.

She's beyond nice. She's beautiful and sweet. Her touch almost makes me want to cry, she's so beautiful.

Her heart is beautiful, too. That's what makes her so intoxicating. She touches me in ways that make me think she actually cares—because she does.

She gets out of the truck without waiting for me to open the door for her. Should I? Are we in the kind of relationship where I should open the door for her?

She might be offended if I wanted to open the door for her. Maybe she doesn't believe in men opening doors for women.

It's too late because she's already getting out. I get out, too.

She waits for me to go in front of her and unlock the house. I do hold the door open for her then, but I can hardly bring myself to make eye contact with her. We're back at my house and that can only mean one thing.

I put my keys on the kitchen counter the way I always do. She walks in as far as the kitchen. She doesn't go any further. She doesn't want to trespass even though I want her here. Don't I? I brought her here. That must mean I want her here.

I'm going to do it with her here. What am I saying? I already did it with her here. I wouldn't have brought her here for anything else—except that we're supposed to be friends.

We aren't friends—not anymore. We're something else. Just don't ask me what we are instead.

I approach her slowly. I don't know what to do about her being here in my house.....and yet I know exactly what to do about her being here in my house.

I want to tear her apart. I want to hear her scream the way she did last night, but I can take my time with that.

Seeing her standing here in my living room somehow means more. Not doing it with her—or at least delaying doing it with her—it means something.

Walking up to her extra slowly.....watching her squirm when she sees me looking at her.....feeling the tension crackle between us....

I don't want this to end. I want it to end and yet I want it to continue. I want to prolong this feeling. I'm going to do it with her, but I can hold myself back as much as I want to.

What is this—this feeling of control? I control everything about this. I control how turned on she gets. I can control that aching, dripping throb between her legs simply by taking a step closer or farther away.

I can control her with the way I look at her. I control her breath. I can make her gasp and catch her breath by glaring at her in smoldering desire......or I can make her relax by looking away or smiling at her in a casual, friendly way.

Everything that happens between us is up to me.

She trembles when I get too close. She trembles with desire.

Her lips sag open and she pants in short, quick gasps. She wants it. She wants me.

She wants me to take her apart exactly the way I want to.....and yet she wants me to control her like this. I sense that.

She surrenders to every shade of my control no matter what I do. I don't even have to touch her to make her crumble. She's already mine......and yet she's so out of reach.

I stop in front of her, but she's too nervous and uncertain about me. She knows I'd never hurt her, but I don't want her to stand here dying of anticipation.

I close my hands around her angelic face and her hair gets messed up again. She's so damn beautiful. Her hair brushes my face when I kiss her.

That kiss gets deeper, hotter, more demanding—not just from me. She grasps at me and prods my mouth open searching for my tongue.

God, I love feeling how much she wants it, but she'll never cross the line to taking back my control. That's all mine and she wants it that way.

I push her back against the kitchen counter. Her hands fly to the counter on either side of her hips to steady herself. Then her hands fly back to my shoulders and chest as we kiss.

I love those little desperate, hopeless gestures of sweet yielding acceptance that I'm in charge. She can't stop me and she doesn't want to.

She grasps at my shoulders. Her fingertips dig into my muscles. Being so much bigger than she is, being so much stronger than she is—it makes her irresistibly tempting.

Knowing I can dismantle her in minutes makes it so much more enthralling to take my time and leave her breathless from wanting me.

She moans when I squeeze her breasts through her shirt. She arches her back, leans a little farther backward over the counter, and shoves her breasts into my hands while she convulses with desire. She's rising again.

I scoop her up under the armpits, sit her on the counter, and push her knees apart. I can't get to her like this—not when she's still wearing her uniform, but that only makes me hotter and harder for her.

Even this painful hot bulge between my legs makes this whole experience so much better. I can wait. I can control when I do it with her and when I finish. I control when I satisfy myself and how. All of that is mine.

I can give her one earth-shattering climax after another. I can keep going all damn night and never get tired. I can spend every hour of every day drinking her sweet nectar.

When I take care of myself or how isn't important. I'll get there eventually and enjoy myself along the way.

I pull her thighs around either side of my waist. She responds to that position as never before. She can't get enough of me between her legs.

She arches into me trying to reach my shaft, but we're both fully dressed. I don't even really want to undress her—not yet. I want to savor this feeling that every breath, every sigh, and every moan is just for me.

She runs her fingers through my hair while we kiss. I clasp both my hands behind her ass and pull her to the very edge of the counter just like I really was going to take her this way.

I want to take her this this. I want to put this on the list of places and positions I'll take her all over this house.

This house means something completely different when I think of it like that. All the work that went into it, all the accomplishments that surround me on every side—could they all have been leading to this?

Could each of them come to represent a place and position where I bent her over and tapped her ass to make her scream my name?

Could each one come to represent her dripping saturated surrender to my hands, my body, and my desires?

I want that. I want this house to mean that. I wasn't just building a nice place to live by myself. I was building all those moments with her—all the sights of her bare breasts in my face and her ass pointed up at me just begging me to own it.

Just because, I scoop her all the way off the counter and hold her up in my arms still kissing her. She wraps her arms even more desperately around my neck to hold onto me. She doesn't try to fight my control—never. She welcomes it.

She doesn't put her legs around my waist, either. She keeps her knees cocked back like she's riding me even though she's too far away.

I stand there in the middle of the living room holding her up and kissing her endlessly. I can stand here forever, just feeling this feeling that she's mine to do exactly as I please.

She won't fight me. She wants me to. She wants to give herself to me and feel that I'm the one doing all of this. Her eyes and lips and body tell me so.

It almost means more when I decide just to prove my power by putting her down. I lower her legs to the floor, make sure she's standing up and supporting her own weight, and I pull off her mouth.

I smile down at her. This feeling gives me such a rush of happiness that I can't help beaming at her. I can stop and start as I please. No one makes me do anything. No one controls me.

I still see the brewing passion in her eyes. She'll be there waiting when I come back and decide to take her there again.

I plan to take her there again. I plan to take her a thousand places again and again and again. I don't even care anymore if it means anything or if she's just enjoying herself with me. I'll enjoy it either w ay.

"Are you hungry?" I ask. "Do you want something to drink?"

I walk away to the fridge, pull it open, and rummage around for something to drink. I don't keep booze in the house, but I have juice, soda, and iced tea.

She already knows that. She says, "Thanks," behind me. I don't look to see her reaction.

I don't have to look. She's still simmering with insatiable, gnawing desire. I can feel the heat radiating off her from here.

I pour her a glass of iced tea and pull out the leftover fajita mix from two days ago. I need to eat, too. Last night took a lot out of me and I haven't fully recovered yet.

Tonight promises to be another marathon. We'll need fuel. I do my best not to smirk to myself thinking that.

Chapter 12: Billy

Brooke wanders into to my living room and looks through the big windows at my backyard garden. "It really is amazing what you've done with this place. I remember what it looked like when you first bought it."

"That was ages ago," I agree. "I would feel ashamed of myself if I left it like that."

She turns around to study my new coffee table. Then her eyes flick up to me when I bring over her tea and a plate of fajitas. It's big enough for both of us to share.

I put down a placemat and bring my own drink before I sit down.

"Did you hear Keith and Leila named their baby boy Leon?" I ask and take a bite out of one of the fajitas. "What are the odds he'll be another firefighter? Leon Brewer. He sounds like a firefighter already."

She starts to smile at me and then sits down next to me on the couch. She takes a sip of her drink and starts eating. "How are you so good at everything, Billy?"

My head shoots up. "Huh? I'm not good at everything. I'm a klutz. You know that."

"You are not. Look at this place. These fajitas are some of the best I've ever had—better than most restaurants. You're good at everything. You always have been."

I look away. "I'm not good at everything. I can barely keep the lights on."

She glances at me and then her eyes range around my house. She sees all the furniture I've made, all the trees and flowerbeds I've planted in the garden, the deck, the hot tub, the kitchen appliances.....

I don't want any of that to change the way I see myself. I would be digging ditches if I didn't become a firefighter.

As it is, I'm one of the lowest ranked firefighters in the whole crew. She knows that. I'll never be a senior like Keith or a city hero like Danny.

I don't want that, either. I'm happy here at the bottom where I belong.

My job is to support them, especially the paramedics. I just do what they tell me to do and get paid. I am definitely not good at everything. I'm not even good at my job. I'm not even average. I'm practically their intern.

They would never say so, but everyone knows it. Brooke is way too nice to ever say something like that, but if she was really honest with herself, she would admit that she knows it, too.

She finishes her fajita and picks up her tea glass to take another drink. Sitting here next to her—it almost feels like we're friends again.

I could be. I could forget the whole thing about doing it with her....and all the places in this house I could do it with her.

In that moment, I can control that, too. I can go back to being friends with her. It won't drive me crazy—except when I think about touching her, kissing her, and feeling her against me.

I can save those moments for when I'm alone. She never has to know.

I take another swig of my tea and pick up my second fajita. "Eat up," I tell her. "Don't leave me to finish these on my own."

She shoots me a smirk on the side. "You need it. You're a growing boy."

I laugh. It feels good to just let the tension dissolve for a change. Does that mean she can let it go, too?

My fajita starts to leak. I bend over the plate to catch the drips.....and that's when she moves in on me.

She doesn't try to stop me from eating. She leans in close, buries her face in my neck from the side, and her hand slips between my thighs.

She grips me hard and immediately makes me start swelling again. Her hot breath stabs into my brain. I have to fight not to choke on my fajita.

I pretend to keep eating—at least until I finish the food in my mouth. Her lips won't let me, though.

Her other hand slips under my T-shirt and she gropes me all over my back, under my armpits, over my shoulders, and around to my chest and stomach.

I put down the rest of my fajita as casually as I can and turn to kiss her. She doesn't wait that long. She dives for me and attacks my mouth. She lunges for me so hard she drives me sideways onto the couch cushions.

She climbs on top of me to straddle me, but I'm still chewing my food. She sticks her tongue in my mouth, tastes the food, and snorts with laughter.

"Didn't you get enough of your own?" I ask.

She straightens up, but she won't stop grinding on my hard bulge. I shove it into her, but that only delights her more. She grins down at me with a glow of blushing sex shining off her cheeks.

"They were really good fajitas," she tells me and starts tugging my T-shirt up to pull it off.

I have to partially sit up to rip it over my head. As soon as I settle back on the cushion, she starts touching my chest again. She corkscrews her hips in circles and her eyes keep blurring out as waves of pleasure sweep through her.

"I was hungry, too," I tease. "You kept me up all night last night. I need to recharge."

She bends down, nibbles my neck, and starts working her mouth down my chest. "No one's stopping you."

"Then you won't mind if I keep eating." I pretend to lean over to pick up my plate.

She bursts out laughing. "Jerk."

"I'm just an innocent bystander here." I lift my plate, put it on my chest above her head, and take another bite.

She snickers. "I bet I can make you stop thinking about food."

"Do your worst, sweetheart. There never was a woman born who could make me stop thinking about food."

She giggles to herself, burrows a little lower down my stomach, and buries her face between my legs. I still have my pants on, but she can feel how hard I am.

She's right. She can make me stop thinking about food. She unzips my uniform pants, pulls my boxers down, and exposes my shaft just enough to get the damn thing into her mouth.

I stop myself from gasping, but I can't stop myself from tensing and spasming as she starts to suck. Holy Christ! I'm gonna die here.

She won't stop inhaling me as she inches my pants down. She sinks onto me all the way and her tongue teases me to the brink of destruction.

I'm supposed to be the one controlling this, but she's enjoying herself too much. I can't bring myself to rob her of the pleasure.

She bathes my rod in her sizzling hot saliva and I feel her throat relax to take me in. I suck my breath through my teeth when her wicked little fingers close around my balls.

I want to do so many things to her, but right now, I satisfy myself with stroking her hair. That doesn't seem like enough, so I grab a fistful of it just because. The sight of her down there taking me in her mouth blows me out of my mind. I've never seen anything so damn hot.

She melts in my grip. Her throat relaxes even more and I increase the pressure—just a little bit. I guide her down a little faster, but she responds perfectly. I can't hold out much longer. I have to pull back.

"You want that, baby?" I growl at her. "You need that? Huh? Is that what you need?"

Her deep green eyes float open to look up at me. I'm the one who needs her. I need everything she's doing to me and everything she wants me to do to her. I'm the one who can't live without this.

She sucks a little faster....a little deeper.....

Just when I think I can't hold on a second longer, she climbs off, crawls up to kiss me, and straddles me again.

I don't have to do anything. She pulls off her T-shirt and sits in front of me in her lacy red bra. It shows off her cleavage right in front of my face.

Then, just in case I thought I might be in a dreamworld or something, she unbuttons her pants, rises on her knees, and scoots them down over those magnificent hips of hers.

She kicks them off along with her work boots, flicks off her bra, stretches out on top of me, and starts kissing me for the ages.

She keeps her legs straight and parallel to mine. She can feel how hard I am and I can feel her juicy nectar staining her ivory-white thighs, but neither of us takes it any further—not yet.

I just want to lie here and kiss her. She's so immaculately beautiful—especially because she doesn't hold back on showing me how much she wants me.

I stroke her body from the back of her neck, down her spine, to the perfect globe of her ass.

I let my fingers trail through the crack between her thighs and around to the squashed pillows of her breasts compressed against my chest. Every inch of her carries me away to heaven.

I don't even have to do it with her to feel this way. That's the most amazing part in all this. We haven't even done it yet.

We did it last night, but we haven't done it today. We don't even need to do it today.

We will, though. I know that now.

This feels so good, so right. I don't want it to end, but I know it will.

She finally manages to tear herself away from my mouth, sits up, and straddles me the way she was before except that she's naked now.

She only smiles at me while I fondle her breasts, stroke her sides and thighs, and follow the slow, delicious spirals of her hips on top of me.

Her cheeks flush with pleasure. I've never seen her like this—so radiant and obviously happy. "Are you sure you don't want to finish your lunch?" she asks.

"You can be my lunch," I tell her.

She bursts into another beaming grin. "You're a growing boy, remember? Having me for lunch won't keep you going."

"Oh, yes, it will. It definitely will. I could show you."

"How would you do that?"

I don't need any clearer invitation than that. I lift her off me. She's so small I can lift her easily.

I stand her in front of me while I swivel sideways to sit frontways on the couch. She complies with everything until she's standing there in front of me waiting for me to do whatever I'm going to do.

I don't need food or water or even air to breathe when I have this. I take hold of her hips and bring her sweet, frilly, swollen petals to my mouth.

She squeals with a sudden rush of pleasure and then her cries spike off the charts as I start to eat her. She sways and almost falls.

I hold her up by her hips and ass while I satisfy myself with devouring her in every luscious mouthful.

She throws back her head and screams. Her fruity juices gush into my mouth and her flesh tastes heavenly.

Her thighs tremble on either side of my face. She can't hold herself up like this.

I take hold of her hands and arms, draw her down on the coffee table without losing contact with her, and lean in to feast myself on every quivering bite.

She stretches back. Her beautiful body sprawls on the coffee table I spent so many painstaking hours sanding to velvet smoothness.

Now I know why I put so much effort into it. Now I know why it had to be so perfect. I didn't know then.

She must sense it. She arches her back, raises her arms above her head, and spreads her thighs extra wide so I can dive all the way in.

Her honeyed perfection covers my face up to my eyelids. My hands on her thighs leave the imprint of my grasping clutches. I was here. I owned this. I devoured this and made her sob and rock in tormented agony as she climaxes again and again.

I'll never stop—not ever. I'll keep her there in the clouds. Her screams will be my music forever—for as long as I still have the breath to satisfy myself with her.

Her hands appear on my head. Her fingers clench in my hair and she raises her legs to rest her feet on my shoulders. Hell yes. Come on, baby. That's right. You can't get enough of this, can you?

She writhes on the coffee table taking it. She shrieks and contorts all over the place when I slide my fingers inside her as I tease her hard little clit to twitching, quivering ecstasy.

I hear her screaming my name—that screaming voice calling to me out of my hottest fantasies. I'll never forget that sound.

Her sauce smears all over her thighs and runs down her ass. I really hope it stains the coffee table. I hope it leaves a permanent mark so I can always remember this moment.

I lift out of her to catch a breath through my nose. Her scent leaves my head reeling in drunken rapture.

I glance up at her and see the curves of her stomach, hips, breasts, and arms all the way up to her face looking down at me.

Her eyebrows knit together in the middle. Her mouth falls open in a desperate panting howl of wild torment.

She looks so impossibly hot like this that I have to take her. I have to take her all the way. I can't let today end without that.

I know she wants it. She wants all of me and everything I can do to her.

I rise on my knees and she falls back on the table staring up at me out of some other dimension. The practical, easy-going paramedic I know isn't home anymore.

This is some wild nymph from the forgotten wasteland of imagination. This is some goddess out of my fevered adolescent wet dreams.

I kneel by the coffee table, but she doesn't move except to lay herself out in front of me with her legs spread. Damn, she wants it bad!

She extends her hands to touch my chest, but I don't see that. I grasp her hips and pull her to the edge of the table—right where I can see every inch of my shaft gliding into her silky wetness.

She raises her arms above her head again and thrusts her breasts up where I can see her taut nipples all ready for me.

I cup my hands under the raised part of her back and stroke into her in a steady, easy rhythm.

She clamps her eyes shut at the first deep penetration. Then her eyes float open and she watches me towering above her.

I stay upright. I could bend over and kiss her, but I want to see her like this. I want to see her gasping, panting, whining, and her eyes rolling back in their sockets when I thump my veiny meat into her.

Her puffy swollen channel spasms around me every time I drive in. Her muscles clench at the limit of my stroke.

That tight squeeze translates all the way down to my nuts. My prick strains to get deeper inside her even though I can't get any deeper than this.

Her hips flare under my hands where her small waist meets her thighs spread for me to enter. Her damp skin spanks into my hips when I thrust in harder.

Her head falls back and her moans turn to cries. She doesn't try to touch me again. She bumps to my rhythm taking me as deep and hard as I want to take her.

She rocks and doesn't try to focus her eyes anymore. She floats in some other world.

Her face transforms into an angelic picture of blissful ecstasy as she screams again and again in broken roars of primal satisfaction.

I feel myself nearing the breaking point, but I don't need to hold back anymore. I want to unload into her. I want....

In that moment, I realize I want to plant my seed in her. She never said anything about using protection. What if she gets pregnant?

That thought skyrockets me out of this world. I want that more than anything.

I want something incredible to grow out of this. I want to feel my seed gushing out of her as I flood her with my essence.

I want to feel her body taking me and growing me into something bigger—bigger than either of us.

I'm not thinking rationally. I can't think rationally with her inner muscles rippling up and down my shaft in electric waves. They milk the deepest drops of my being from me and I erupt inside her.

The heat pouring out of her makes me bellow in all this tortured passion. I don't understand what's happening to me. This......this is taking over my life in ways I don't understand, but it's already happening.

My innermost soul ejects into her. I'll never get it back and I don't want to. I want it to live there and grow there. I want her to harbor me and keep me safe in that dark place where only I can go.

She screams at the same time and arches all the way back on the table to take me as deep and hard as I can possibly thrust into her. Her screams join with mine in some call to the universe to make this happen even though I know it's impossible.

Chapter 13: Billy

Brooke lies in my arms on my bed again. We're both naked and exhausted from hours of non-stop sex, but this time, we lie under the covers to keep us warm.

"Are you awake?" she whispers in my ear.

"No," I tell her.

She giggles. "Always the comedian."

"It's my only way to get people to like me."

Her hand moves down my chest. "Stop it," she whispers.

She seems obsessed with my chest. She won't stop stroking me and running her fingers through my hair all the way down to my stomach.

I always catch her looking at my body, too, and she doesn't look away—so why did she look away that first morning? Could it be that she likes the way I look?

Maybe she just didn't feel comfortable checking me out then. I wouldn't have felt comfortable with her checking me out, either. I wouldn't have felt comfortable with anything that morning.

"Do you want to finish your fajitas now?" she asks.

I snort. "I told you I would have you for lunch. I don't need food."

She snickers again. "You're going to get hungry."

"Hungry for you." I kiss her on the cheek, but I don't take it any further.

My prick hurts from doing it so much—not in a friction-rugburn kind of way—more of an aching, drained kind of way. I can just imagine what she feels like. Her most sensitive tissues have gotten one hell of a workout the past two nights.

She keeps trembling at odd times as shivers of energy pass through her. She cuddles close to me each time this happens.

I can't get enough of the feeling of her huddling in my arms for protection—protection from her own insatiable desires.

Even now, I can feel that she still wants me. She keeps gliding her thighs over my leg and pressing her stomach and pelvis against me. I feel her juices on her thighs, but she doesn't take it further, either.

I settle down on the pillows and run my fingers through her hair. I keep my eyes closed so I can take in every blissful sensation of her lying here.

How much longer can this go on? Neither of us has to work today. We can keep doing this all day and all night tomorrow night, but what about after that?

She'll have to go home eventually and that's not saying anything about both of us needing to go to work at some point.

She must be thinking the same thing. She nuzzles up into my neck and murmurs, "Thank you for tonight—and last night."

I kiss her hair again. "I'm glad you liked it."

"You know I liked it. You're the best I've ever had."

I raise my eyebrows and try to look down at her, but it's kinda hard when she's lying so close. "I am? That's impossible. Someone out there must be better than me."

"I'm sure someone is, but they aren't here. You're incredible—amazing."

"I don't know anything," I tell her. "I'm just making it up."

"You can make it up with me anytime." She kisses me under my ear. "I've never had it like this before."

I allow my hand to travel up to the back of her neck and kiss her on the lips this time. "I've never had it like this before, either, but we won't be able to do it again. We agreed we'd stay friends."

Her tone changes. "Yeah. I know."

"That's what you wanted, isn't it? Isn't that what we agreed in the parking lot—that we wouldn't let it happen again.?

"But we did let it happen again."

"Let's call it a tragic accident."

She starts off by laughing again. "This is serious. It wasn't an accident—unless I fell off the bus and just happened to land here in your bed."

"Okay, it wasn't an accident, but that doesn't mean it has to happen again."

"But we said at the parking lot that it wouldn't happen and it did happen again. If we say now that it won't happen again, it could happen again the same way it happened this time."

I try to shrug it away. This conversation is going in a direction it shouldn't. "We said in the parking lot that our friendship is more important. If not doing it again is what it takes for us to be friends, then that's what we have to do. That's what we agreed, isn't it?"

She settles down again. "Yeah. We did."

"That's what you want, isn't it—for us to be friends? It beats tiptoeing around each other in awkward silence—especially since we have to work together."

"Yeah," she murmurs. "It's better if we don't."

"It's the smart thing to do," I tell her. "Things were fine before this started."

She doesn't say anything for a while. I could drift off right now, but this feels too good. I don't want to go to sleep if this is going to be the last time. I want to stay awake for every delicious minute.

Her voice floats out of the darkness. "Is that what you want?"

"If that's what you want, then that's what I want," I tell her. "I don't want something you don't want."

She shoots off the bed, props herself on her elbow, and stares down at me. Those eyes glisten with something deeper than sex.

"You.....would you want something else—something more than that?"

I look away. "I didn't say that."

"Answer me, Billy!" she snaps. "Do you want more than that—more than friendship—more than just hooking up and forgetting about it?"

I can't look at her. "I just told you. I don't want anything you don't want. If you want to be friends—or even friends with benefits—that's fine with me."

She doesn't move. Is she even breathing?

She stares down at me for so long that I really start to get scared. What is wrong with her?

"You want that, don't you?" she whispers. "You want more."

I open my mouth to speak, but no sound comes out. I can't say it. I can't tell her what I saw and felt while we were doing it on the coffee table.

I can't tell her how intoxicatingly, electrifyingly tempting it was to feel like I was getting her pregnant—that we could be something that serious.

I can't tell her. She doesn't want to hear that—especially not from a guy like me. This is just some fun for her—and she's too smart to think anything else.

I'm not that guy—not to her or any other woman. I'm the guy women avoid doing all of that with.

She won't leave it alone. "Could we be like that, Billy?" she whispers. "Could we be.....more?"

"Don't talk like that, baby." I hear my voice shaking. I can't be talking to her about this.

"If I said I wanted it, would you want it?" she asks. "You just said you don't want anything I don't want. What if I told you I wanted it, too? Would you say you wanted it, too? What if we both want it?"

"We both don't want it. You said you wanted to be friends."

"You said it, too!" she points out. "You said we should just let it go."

"You were the one who said we shouldn't let it happen again. Then you were the one who started touching me again. I wouldn't have done anything. You were the one who did that."

"That's because I want you!" she blurts out. "I only said we wouldn't let it happen again because I thought that's what you wanted."

I spin around and my eyes snap open. "You did?"

"Of course! Of course I want to do it again! Do you think I didn't enjoy it or something?"

"So....what does that mean? Does that mean you stop by for sex every now and then?"

"NO!!" she shrieks. "Tell me straight up if you want this to turn into something.....something serious. Tell me right now."

I open my mouth again, and again, words fail me. I can't say that. I can't say I want it to turn into something serious even though I do. I want that more than anything.

I want everything I saw on the coffee table—everything I felt. I could never tell her that, though.

"You do, don't you?" she murmurs. "You want it."

I gulp and force myself to look away.

"Did you only say that because you thought that's what I wanted?"

I nod at the wall. I can't look at her.

She sinks onto the bed—back into my arms. I can't relax. This isn't happening. I didn't just tell her my deepest, darkest secret.

She lies there breathing into my chest for a while. I hardly dare to touch her now. This whole thing is about to blow up in my face in the worst possible way.

She doesn't relax, either—not the way she did before. What is she thinking? Is she planning how she can get the hell out of my bed, out of my house, and out of my life as tactfully as possible? That's what I'd be doing if I was in her place.

After way too long, she tilts her head back and looks up at me. "So....how do we do it?"

"How do we do what?"

"Have a relationship with each other. Go out with each other. Get involved with each other. Get serious about each other."

My head whips around again. The bottom drops out from under my world. "You can't be serious!"

"Why not? You said you wanted it and I want it. You said you only wanted to be friends because you thought that's what I wanted. I said the same thing. If we both want it...."

"No!" I counter. This feeling of flying apart at the seams rockets me off the bed.

I realize I'm pushing her away too roughly, but I can't stay in bed with her—not like this.

She falls off me onto the mattress when I sit up. I grab my pajama pants and slip them on before I stand up.

"Hey—wait!" she calls after me. "What's wrong? Where are you going?"

"We are not doing that!" I snap over my shoulder.

"Why not? We both want it...."

"Wanting it and having it aren't the same thing. You don't know what you're asking."

"Why can't you at least explain it to me? How else am I supposed to understand?"

"You don't want to get involved with me, okay?" I reply over my shoulder and head for the door.

"I just said I did! Hey!"

She doesn't get out of bed to come after me. She stays there all warm and naked and beautiful in my bed.

Jesus, what the hell is wrong with me? I never should have let this happen. I shouldn't have let her get attached to me. That was my mistake.

I go out to the living room and sit on the couch stewing in torment while I drink the rest of my tea that I left on the coffee table. It's still sitting there since Brooke and I first got back from the firehouse.

My leftover fajitas are still sitting there, too, but I can't eat. My stomach hurts.

She does NOT want to get involved with me. Hell no.

Chapter 14: Billy

I'm still sitting here in front of my uneaten fajitas when Brooke comes out of the bedroom. She walks around the living room picking up her clothes and putting them on. Of course. She knows now that I'm no good for her, so it's time to leave.

The only clothes she has to wear are her uniform clothes from work today. She even puts on her boots.

She doesn't leave right away, though. As soon as she gets fully dressed, she sits down in the leather armchair across the coffee table from me.

"I just want you to know," she begins, "that I really do want this. I won't push you to do something that you obviously don't want. Just make sure you know we aren't doing this because you don't want to. It isn't because I don't want it because I do. I need you to tell me right now that you don't want it. Then I'll walk out that door and we never have to have this conversation again, but I need you to tell me right now that you don't want to go through with this. If you do want to go through with it, I'm all in. If you don't, I'll walk away. It's that simple."

I blink at her trying to understand the words she just said. "You're serious. You really want this."

"Of course I do!" she blurts out. "We've been close for years. I care about you and I know you care about me. We get along better than anyone else in my life and the sex was phenomenal. What could be wrong with that?"

I look away. "A lot could be wrong with it."

"I don't believe you," she snaps. "You want this as much as I do. I just can't figure out why you're pushing me away...."

"I'm not pushing you away," I tell her. "You're the one threatening to walk out on me...."

"Threatening!" she fires back. "You won't even explain why you can't do it."

I shut my mouth and distract myself by drinking another mouthful of tea, but that makes me sick, too. "I can't."

"Then what more is there to say? Why should I stay if you don't want to do it?"

"I do want to do it!" I yell back.

I fight my voice under control. I feel myself losing it.

She stares at me for a second before I realize I just said I want to do it. I can't even think about what I just said I want to do.

Have a relationship with each other? Go out with each other? Get involved with each other? Get serious about each other?

My mind reels off into another tailspin just thinking about it. Holy crap, do I want that, but I could never have it—not with a woman as good as Brooke Elsworth. Not in my wildest dreams.

Before I know what's happening, she comes over and sits down on the couch next to me. I fiddle with the tea glass and run my finger through the ring of water on the placemat so I don't have to look at her.

She slips her delicate little hand into mine. My hand dwarfs hers, but her hand feels somehow so much more powerful and self-assured than mine.

She threads her fingers into mine. "Do you want to go out some-time?"

"What do you mean by 'out'?" God only knows why I'm even asking.

"You know—like on a date."

"You mean sit across from each other in a romantic restaurant and look at each other?"

"And talk to each other. Isn't that what people do on dates?"

I snort. "That sounds the most uncomfortable, awkward thing I can possibly imagine."

She snickers under her breath. "Then we could fly our spaceships around the grocery store seeking out new life and new civilizations."

I can't help laughing. "That isn't a date. That's just us being friends and being stupid."

"You're right," she murmurs. "What should we do instead?"

I look over at her. This isn't happening. We aren't having this conversation. It scares the living shit out of me, but her eyes shine up at me with so much warmth and understanding that a brick falls into my stomach.

"You really want to do this, don't you?" I can barely make myself heard. "Like—for real?"

"Yeah!" she whispers back and bursts into a huge grin. "It could be great."

"It could be a disaster."

"Wouldn't it be worth it to find out?"

"You could wind up hating me," I mutter under my breath.

"I would never hate you." She leans in and kisses the side of my face. "So....are you okay with it?"

"I guess so....if it's what you want."

She leans back to study me. "You would do it because I want it? You would do it to give me what I want?"

"Of course. You know I'd do anything for you."

She doesn't beam or even grin at me. She just gazes at me like she's trying to figure me out or something.

Her gaze makes me uncomfortable. I want to squirm.

Of course I'd do it to make her happy—for as long as it lasts. She'll figure out pretty soon what a terrible idea this is. Then she'll move on.

If this is what it takes to convince her, then I guess I can go along with it.

She leans back on the couch, but she doesn't stop holding my hand. "So what do you want to do first?"

"Besides tear your clothes off? That's about it."

She laughs. "If you don't want to date, we could just move to the old-married-couple stage of the relationship."

"You mean where we hate each other? We can do that now without getting involved."

"Don't talk like that," she murmurs. "I meant where we already know everything about each other and we still like each other and want to be together. We don't have to date. We can just call it good and say we're already involved with each other—which is kinda true, don't you think? It isn't like we need to get to know each other or anything."

I look up at her. She's really doing this. She wants to—because she wants me.

She's right that we already know each other. She knows me better than anyone. Taking her out to romantic restaurants wouldn't change that.

She lets go of my hand and starts raking her fingertips up and down my bare back. That feeling electrifies me, but I hold myself under control. This isn't the time for that, but I sure wish it was. I want to tackle her again.

"So how was your day at work today?" she asks.

"Ask me that with your shirt off."

Don't ask me why I said that. It just slipped out. I just don't know how to talk to her anymore—not with this hanging over my head.

I have no flippin' clue how to start being involved with her. I don't know how to date her or have a relationship with her or how to get serious about her even though I already am in every way that counts.

I don't expect her to take my answer seriously, but she does.

She pulls off her shirt, flicks off her bra, shimmies out of her pants, and kicks off her boots.

I watch in stunned amazement as she climbs onto my lap and straddles me on the edge of the couch—right where she'll sit with her breasts in my face.

She wraps her arms around me and rocks her sweet box against me through my pajama pants. She shoves her breasts right in my face.

"So...." She lets out a little tortured gasp as her hair spills over her face in another rush of passion. "How was your.....ah!.....How was....your day?"

She pants faster as her energy rises. My arms float around her and I lock her against me. I want her so unbelievably badly. I need to own her and take her and keep her. I can't do that unless we really are seriously involved.

I caress up her back, grab her hair, pull her head back, and maul her breasts in my mouth. "There's this really hot paramedic there," I tell her between bites and sucks on her nipples. "She put her arms around me on our last call and touched my hands and everything."

She squeals when I bite her and then moans when I suck the pain away. I grab one of her breasts, squeeze it hard to make the nipple stand out stiff and taut, and then hold it like that while I torture it to the limit.

She screams and tries to thrash out of my grip, but I don't let her go. I hold her like that and savor the sweet cries rising to shrieks.

"I think I'll corner her in the locker room, bend her over the bench, strip down her pants, and nail her right there," I snarl under my breath. "I think I'll take her home, lock her in my bedroom, strip her, tie her up, and make her mine forever."

She's screaming too loudly to answer. I let go of her breasts and let my hands trail down her hourglass sides to her voluptuous ass rocking on my lap.

"She looks so hot in her uniform and turnouts," I growl. "I bet she tastes just as good when she spreads her legs."

I tiptoe my fingers lower to the crack of her ass.....and lower to her molten slit. She's already dripping wet and soaking through my pajamas.

"What do you think, baby?" I growl. "Do you think some hot paramedic from Howe Firehouse would like it if I teased her sweet flower with my fingers and then plowed her until she screams? Do you think she would like that?"

"Yes!!" she screams. "Yes!!"

"Do you think she would scream my name and beg me to take her?" I ask no one in particular. "Do you think she'd back up that juicy round ass for me to pound her into my coffee table?"

"YES!!" she roars. "YES!!"

"Say my name, baby," I tell her.

Just to make it more complicated, I swirl my fingers in her juices and rub them up to her clit. I don't have to do it with her. I can take her to the stars just by sitting here minding my own business.

"BILLY!!" she screams. "BILLY—PLEASE!"

"Billy, please what?" I demand. "What are you asking me to do, baby?"

She screams one more time, "PLEASE....." before words fail her. She falls apart screaming and spasming in my arms as she dissolves in another brutal climax.

She clings to me screaming in my ear, but I don't do anything else.

She's so precious to me. She's the only woman who actually wants to be like this with me....and she wants more. She wants us to be for real.

Thinking that hurts. I want so much more with her. I just don't want to hurt her in the process.

Chapter 15:
Brooke

I unbuckle my seatbelt, lean across the seat in the cab of Billy's truck, and kiss him. "You have a good day at work today, okay, dear?"

He snorts. "You, too, honeycakes. Try to stay out of trouble, okay?"

I smirk at him and open the passenger door. He throws the truck into *Park,* sets the emergency brake, and gets out, too. We're both on shift this morning, so all this saying-goodbye-to-each-other-before-work is just a joke.

He takes his duffel bag out of the back, shuts the driver's door, and locks his truck. I walk around the truck to join him on our way into the firehouse.

It's been three days since we decided to....do whatever it is we decided to do.

I don't even really know what to call it except that we aren't friends anymore. We aren't exactly a couple because no one else knows about us. Even we don't know about us.

We're doing something, though. We're going on with this as something more than sex on the side.

We're still having plenty of that, but we decided to spend more time at our own separate residences so we actually get some sleep.

I spent last night at my apartment before he picked me up for work this morning. I have no idea when I'll go back to his house or if or when he'll come to my apartment.

Staying at his house and doing it all night long feels so natural now. Everything about this feels natural and easy and inevitable. I can't believe it took so long for us to get here.

We walk into the firehouse and go straight to the locker room. No one even notices us showing up together.

"When are you gonna bring that baby in for all of us to slobber over?" Ellis asks Keith.

"Never," Keith growls. "You will never slobber over my baby. I can promise you that right now, pal."

"At least bring him in so we can all admire him," Naomi tells him. "We're dying here."

"He's just a baby," Danny points out. "You've all seen babies a million times. What's so special about this one?"

"He's a firehouse baby," Danny's wife Emily tells him.

"*You* don't need to see him," Danny replies. "You've already seen him when we visited Leila in the hospital."

"No fair!" Chris counters. "How come she's allowed to visit Leila in the hospital and we aren't?"

"You're too late," Keith replies. "She's home now and I sure as hell don't want all you goons rolling up on her. She'll come visit you here when she's ready."

"When will that be?" Chris asks.

He shrugs. "I don't know. I'll tell her you want to see her and Leon. Then she can decide when she's ready to come."

"Leon," Billy repeats. "Great name, man. Real classy."

"Thanks, brother," Keith replies. "I picked it out myself."

"No kidding? I'm impressed."

"What did you think—that I would give him a stupid name like Friedrich or some shit? Give me a little credit."

"Didn't Leila have anything to say about the name?" Drew Killian asks.

"We made a list of our top choices," Keith replies. "Then we whittled it down to two—a girl name and boy name. The boy name won out."

"I think it's an outstanding name," Billy tells him. "He sounds like a champion."

Keith beams at him. "He's a little tiger."

"You would say that," Andy adds. "You're his father."

"Of course Keith says that," Josh points out. "He has every reason to be proud of his son."

"Thanks, man," Keith growls.

Just then, John rolls into the firehouse. "What are we doing?"

"We're talking about Leon," Drew informs him.

John nods. "He's a chip off the old block."

Keith turns bright red. "We made a pact to accept it if he doesn't want to go into emergency services work. We want him to pursue his own interests without any pressure to follow in our footsteps."

"Good for you," John replies. "Oakleigh isn't interested in emergency work, either."

"She's smart," Chris points out. "Emergency work is no picnic."

"Zeke doesn't want to do emergency work, either," Danny adds. "He started out saying he did, but he changed his mind. Now he wants to be a computer engineer."

"He certainly has the brain for it," Sophie remarks.

"He isn't a Brewer, though, is he?" Billy argues. "He's a boy and Oakleigh is a girl. What do you want to bet Leon goes into the family business and becomes a firefighter just like his old man? I bet you anything."

"We have some years ahead of us before we find out." John turns away toward the stairs. "Let's get this done while we wait."

Josh claps Keith on the shoulder. "Give Leila our best."

He walks back to the ambulance where he's working with Naomi today. The rest of us take the hint and get to work, too.

I'm working with Sophie on the rescue truck today. We do a detailed check of our gear. Billy and Danny work in the front going over all the fire-related gear.

Sophie rummages under the seat checking the turnouts. "Hey! Did one of you guys see my BP cuff? I think I left it in the truck last shift."

"I haven't seen it," Danny replies over his shoulder and goes right back to what he was doing.

"I know where it is." Billy stops work, leans over the seat, sticks his head and shoulders under the next seat in front of us, and pulls out Caleb's turnouts.

The bundle falls open and Sophie's BP cuff hits the seat. She pounces on it. "Yay! Thank you so much, Billy! How did you find that?"

"I spotted it yesterday when we were putting the turnouts away. I was gonna take it out and ask whose it was, but then we got that call for the car wreck, so I forgot."

He starts folding up Caleb's turnouts and putting them away.

She sinks onto the seat next to me, winds up the cuff and all its hoses, and sighs with relief. "I was worried I left it at the scene or something."

Billy catches me looking at him over her head. He smiles and then turns away to go back to his own business.

That moment of eye contact sends a thread of fire through my insides. All these people would have plenty to talk about if they knew what Billy and I have been doing at his house these last few days.

None of these people will ever find out, though. Whatever this is going on between me and Billy, it's our secret.

He and Danny get out of the truck and go to work on something else. Sophie and I start going over the drug box.

Josh sticks his head in to ask if he can snag some of our doses because the firehouse drug stores are out. We're in the middle of that conversation when the fire alarm goes off.

He races back to his ambulance and all the firefighters bundle into the truck. "Where are we going?!" Keith yells to Billy.

"Gas leak at the corner of Chestnut Avenue and Morton Road," Billy hollers back over the sirens.

"Gas leak!" Ellis snaps. "Can't we get a real call?"

"You can sit under a tree and crochet a doily while the rest of us go into the house to check for the leak," Billy calls over the seat.

The others laugh. I find myself studying the back of Billy's head while we drive. He's been there right in front of me all this time.

I get a rush of pride for him. He's my....whatever he is. Boyfriend? Date? Lover? I don't know what to call him, but I share something with him that none of these people understand or share.

I hate to call him mine, but I've never been prouder of him. I love his dedication to the job. He always does his best for everyone, especially everyone else on the fire crew.

We pull up in front of the house in question. A family of five stands on the sidewalk—as far away from the house as they can get. The mother holds a little white dog in her arms and hugs her three boys close to her.

"When did you notice the smell?" Keith asks.

"About fifteen minutes ago," the father tells us. "We were having breakfast when we noticed it."

Billy frowns at the guy. "So you were all sitting around having breakfast when you noticed the smell? It just started up without warning?"

The man nods. "Everything was fine before that."

"That's strange," Billy replies. "Something must have caused it."

Keith waves him away. "Let's go check it out. All of you put on your SCBAs. If the smell was that noticeable...."

Before he can say another word, an almighty boom detonates the house. The whole house explodes in a massive fireball.

The blast sends flying timbers, broken glass, and roofing tiles wheeling through the air. Everybody ducks and cowers under their arms.

No one moves for a second as the fire blasts outward and then sucks back in on itself. It woofs into the air before it starts crackling straight up like a normal fire.

The whole wooden house frame pops and hisses in the flames. Every square inch of the house is on fire, just like that.

"Let's go, people!" Keith bellows. "Get those hoses out, Billy! All you paramedics back off and give us some space! Take the ambulances back to the firehouse. Let's go! Get around the other side, Danny!"

Josh, Naomi, Andy, and Drew take the two ambulances back to the firehouse. Sophie and I get stuck at the scene watching Billy, Caleb, Keith, Ellis, and all the guys from the ladder truck pull out their hoses.

The guys hook up their hoses to the city water supply and start hosing down what's left of the house—which isn't very much.

I hold out my arm to the family. "Come on over here and give the crew room to work. You're all safe. That's the important thing."

The woman's lips twist in horrible knots, but she doesn't let herself cry. The boys stare at the fire in dazed shock.

The father does the same thing, but only for a second. "Does one of you have a phone I can use? I need to call my brother about giving us a place to stay tonight."

"Sure," I tell him and hand him my own phone.

He walks away from his family for a few minutes and talks to someone on the other end. The house keeps crackling away just a few dozen yards from where we stand.

I can't do anything else besides support the family. Billy and the guys work around and around the house, but nothing can save it. They work mostly to stop the fire from spreading to the neighboring houses.

I get another overpowering surge of pride watching Billy.

John shows up a few minutes later and interviews me and Sophie about what caused the explosion. I repeat what the family told us about the leak.

"We'll probably never find out what caused it," John tells the father when the guy gets off the phone.

The father only nods. "It doesn't make much difference now, does it? We have a place to stay until we find a more permanent solution. Thank you for all your help."

"I only wish we could do more." John shakes hands with him and leaves. Keith is handling the crew and they're almost done.

The whole house burns down to the foundation by the time they put out the flames completely. The cinders lie there smoldering. The guys go through them dowsing them the rest of the way to put them out.

They only get halfway done before a different man in a business suit pulls up to the curb. The father puts his family in the car and the driver takes off with all five of them. That must be the father's brother.

Now there really is nothing for me and Sophie to do but wait for the guys to pack up their hoses. Sophie and I help out as much as we can, now that the danger is over.

The neighbors who gathered outside to watch and make comments go back to their lives, too, so we can joke around more while we work.

"I'm putting in an order for all our calls to go like this one from now on," Ellis tells Keith.

"All the fun of putting out a fire with no one trapped inside?" Caleb asks.

"Exactly," Ellis replies. "They should all be like this."

"Hey, Mother Theresa," Billy interjects. "How about you put in an order for no one's house to burn down ever again? Why not go all the way?"

Ellis shrugs. "Okay. I'll put in an order for that instead."

"Let's not hold our breath," Sophie chimes in.

"I really need to start going to a different restaurant," Ellis remarks. "The service at this one is terrible. They never get my order right."

The rest of us laugh at him and he grins back at us. We roll back to the firehouse where we hang up the hoses to dry and load on fresh, dry ones so we're ready for our next call.

We don't get one. We finish all our chores and go up to the break room to hang out. Keith, Danny, Josh, and most of the paramedics work on their professional development packages and study for our recertification exams.

"When are you gonna start taking professional development?" Ellis asks Billy.

"What's the point?" Billy asks. "I'm not developing professionally."

"Why not?" Keith asks.

Billy frowns at him. "Why would I want to do that?"

"So you can rise in the ranks and get more training for a higher position."

Billy furrows his brow. He really doesn't understand at all.

The conversation shifts and everyone forgets about Billy's professional development—everyone but me.

Now that I think about it, he never takes professional development. He's the lowest ranked firefighter in the whole Howe Fire Department, but he's been here longer than some of the others.

Caleb and Ellis both joined after Billy. They both outrank him now because they keep passing professional development levels.

He doesn't notice nor does he seem to care. He never even tries. Why?

I always explained it away in the past. I figured he was just happy with his job the way it is. What if I'm wrong? What if there's a reason Billy doesn't want to rise in rank?

He knows by now that the higher ranks earn more money, so that can't be the reason. He could have made more by getting EMT or paramedic certified. He could have had a safer job on the ambulance.

The strange thing is that he takes the same attitude toward professional development that he took toward getting involved with me. He doesn't want to stick his neck out, not even if the potential payoff would be worth the risk.

I can't explain it, but it matters more because I'm involved with him now.

If something is affecting him, I should find out what it is. It might be something serious that could spill over and affect our relationship. In fact, it already is.

I don't like having something unknown hanging over my head—over both our heads. I don't like not knowing something that could risk our whole relationship.

I can't just come out and demand an answer from him. We aren't there yet. Maybe we never will be. Maybe Billy will take this secret to his grave.

Chapter 16:
Brooke

I meet up with Billy outside the locker room. He checks behind me to make sure no one is in there who might overhear us. "Are you coming over tonight?" he asks in a hushed undertone.

My stomach flips. "I don't know. Am I?"

He bursts out in a smirk. "Do you think you can keep your hands off me?"

"No," I reply. "If that's the criteria, then no, I'm not coming over."

He laughs and starts to slip his arm around my waist from behind. "Come over...." He has to pull away when we hear people coming down the stairs.

"I have to go with you because I don't have a car here, remember?" I tell him and head away to the parking lot. "Unless you want me to walk there."

He laughs again, but just then, Keith, Danny, and John come down the stairs. They're all too busy talking to notice anything unusual about me and Billy.

We say goodbye to the three brothers, get in Billy's truck, and drive to his place. "So what's tonight's date?" he asks me.

"You mean we aren't going to tear each other's clothes off? I'm disappointed."

He laughs and flops on the couch. "I think you might have worn me out, sweetheart."

"I bet I can revive you." I sit down next to him and kiss him.

"Old married couples don't screw around like we do. They would break their hips."

"How do you know? You've never been an old married couple. They might be knocking the boots seven times a day for all we know."

He turns bright red, laughs, and holds out his arms to me. "Come lie down here." He guides me down on the couch next to him and puts his arms around me. "Do you want to watch a movie or something before we get to the main event?"

Now it's my turn to laugh. "You really are getting old, aren't you?"

He cranes himself off the couch and grabs the remote from the shelf under the coffee table. "We might see something really explicit and get some new ideas."

He flicks on the TV and starts scrolling. "Your choices are..... *Alien vs. Predator* ......*Despicable Me*......or *Teletubbies*."

"*Teletubbies* isn't a movie," I tell him.

"*Alien vs. Predator* it is, then." He clicks back to the movie, props the remote on the couch behind him, and settles in with me on his chest.

I wrap my arms around him.....and fall sound asleep.

I wake up when sunshine hits me in the eyes. I pry my face off Billy's chest and pretend I didn't leave a damp spot of drool on his T-shirt.

He lies sound asleep on the couch underneath me. This is a repeat of that morning in my apartment except now we're in his house.

Now I know for certain we didn't do it last night. I wasn't drunk, and if we were going to do it, we would have. I wouldn't be lying here in my uniform. Billy is still wearing his, too.

Me lifting my head makes him stir, but he only turns his head aside, sniffs, and goes back to sleep.

The TV is off. He must have either woken up during the night and turned it off or else he realized I was asleep and turned it off before he fell asleep.

I sink back into my place and relax. I don't have to go anywhere.

Lying here with Billy feels so good. We haven't done this before—not like this—not as a couple. It feels good—really good.

I want to wake him up so he sees and feels how good it is, but I don't want to wake him up.

I put my head back down on his chest. The sunshine makes me sleepy and I drift off a second time.

I wake up when Billy coughs. I jolt out of a sound sleep.

"It's all right," he murmurs. "It's nothing."

I take a minute to realize we're still on the couch. Neither of us has moved.

I collapse on his chest and shut my eyes again, but I can't go back to sleep.

He kisses my hair. "Hey, baby," he husks.

I squeeze him tighter. "Hi."

"Did you sleep well?" he asks.

"I passed out. Sorry about that. I missed our date."

His chest rumbles when he chuckles. "I'll just have to make you sit through *Alien vs. Predator* another time."

I burrow deeper into his chest. I don't want to be anywhere else. "This was the nicest date I've ever been on."

He cups my chin and lifts my face to gaze into my eyes. "Nicer than me ripping your clothes off?"

"Much nicer."

He sinks deep into kissing me. Our lips are still tangled together when he murmurs, "It was nicer for me, too."

I lose track of time. Kissing Billy wipes out my awareness of everything but our lips gliding together, our tongues dancing and coiling in an endless rhythm, and this blissful sensation that nothing can ever come between us.

Time does keep going on, though. He finally lets his head fall back on the cushion "So what do you want to do tonight?" he asks me.

"Does that mean we're taking a break knocking the boots?"

"I think both of us probably need to recover. We might put each other in the hospital if this keeps up."

I can only beam at him. Everything he does and says delights me. "Okay. I can live with that."

"So what's Plan B?"

"Bowling?"

His eyes pop. "Great idea!"

"I was joking, sugarplum," I tell him.

"Oh." He frowns. "I like bowling."

Now it's my turn to raise my eyebrows. "You're messing with me, right?"

"Not at all. It's fun. Come on. I haven't gone bowling for ages."

He starts to heave himself off the couch. I don't move.

He stops by the coffee table and frowns at me. "What's wrong?"

"I...."

He bursts into a wild smirk. "Are you worried I'll beat you? I promise I'll let you win."

"I'm not worried you'll beat me. I know you will because I've never gone bowling before."

His jaw hits the carpet. "You what?"

"I've never gone...."

"I heard you! How can you not have gone bowling before?"

I shrug.

"That's it. We're going." He grabs my hand and hauls me off the couch.

"What is it—some kind of Neanderthal mating ritual or something?" I tease.

"Only because of what I'm going to do to you when I get you home. Come on. We can eat when we get there."

"But...." I protest. "We're both still in uniform."

That's the one thing that makes him stop and think about it. "Oh, right," he mumbles and then his expression clears. "I'll change here and then we'll stop by your apartment so you can change before we go." He checks the time. "It's early yet."

I guess he's made his decision. He goes to his bedroom to change out of his uniform. I wander around his house checking out all the stuff he's made, restored, and renovated.

There's no shortage of marvels for me to admire. I know all of them, but I still can't help remarking again how talented he is. So why doesn't he do something with all that buried potential? Why is he so insistent that he's no good for anything or to anyone?

He comes out wearing jeans, sneakers, and a leather jacket over a black T-shirt. These clothes somehow make him seem even bigger, broader, beefier, and even more attractive. I could definitely get on board with ripping those clothes off.

He doesn't notice me eyeing him. He grabs his keys and we go outside. Before I think to stop him or even realize what he's doing, he goes to the truck passenger door and opens it for me.

I'm so shocked I stop dead on the front steps staring at him. He studies me for a second before he blushes to the roots of his sandy blonde hair.

"Sorry," he husks. "It's just a habit."

"You never did it before."

"It just bothered me that you opened the door yourself. Where I come from, a man always opens a door for a lady."

I don't know what to think, but he doesn't leave the passenger door. He nods toward it. "Come on," he murmurs. "Just get in."

I hustle over there, sit down in the seat, and he shuts the door with me inside. Then he gets in and drives to my apartment.

I squirm in my seat. What just happened? Does this mean we're official or what?

He says it always bothered him. Does that mean it bothered him before we started seeing each other?

I don't even know what that means. We never really started seeing each other. We saw each other all the time before all this sex and relationship craziness started. He never opened the door for me then.

Maybe he wanted to, though. Maybe he wanted to and didn't think he could because we weren't actually a couple. Maybe I'm reading way too much into this.

I try not to read too much into him coming into my apartment with me while I change. He doesn't interfere, though. He just waits in the living room.

I have to stop myself from dressing up. This is our first official date even though it isn't an official date. We're just hanging out.

Going bowling with him isn't anything we wouldn't have done before, either. It's exactly the kind of thing we would have done. In fact, everything is exactly the same—except the part about him opening my door.

I decide to dress as casually as he is. I wear the jeans, a T-shirt, and cropped plaid shirt tied under my breasts. He always liked that outfit. It's nice enough and feminine enough to wear on a casual date, but not nice enough to make it seem like I'm making this into something it isn't.

He definitely appreciates it, though. His eyes widen when I go back out to the living room with my hair in a loose ponytail with stray locks hanging on either side of my eyes.

"What a knockout!" he breathes.

I blush and lower my eyes. "Hardly."

"I am going to have a hard time keeping my hands off you in public." He circles my waist and draws me in to kiss me. "That outfit always did piss me off when I saw other guys checking you out."

"I'm sure not nearly as many guys checked me out as you imagined."

"And I'm sure a lot more guys checked you out than you imagined. You thought you were being plain and understated when you were actually the hottest showstopper in the house."

I glance down at my clothes. "Should I change, then? Is it too much?"

"NO!!" he yells. "Don't change anything. Stay exactly like that."

I turn bright red again, but he's already taking my hand and leading me outside.

This time, he holds onto me and leads me to the passenger door. He opens it and sits me inside before we drive into town.

He sure is acting like this is a real date and I guess it is. I guess I just need to wrap my head around the fact that Billy and I are a couple now.

I don't see much difference in the way we act with each other—apart from all the sex.

Oh, and the look in his eyes when he glances over at me at stoplights. That definitely gives it away. This is different.

I catch him gazing at me with deep love, passion, and pride the way I've been gazing at him. His eyes keep dipping appreciatively to my clothes and body. I don't have to wonder what that look means. I know exactly what's going to happen when we finish bowling.

Chapter 17: Brooke

B illy parks in front of the bowling alley and we go inside. I don't know what to do first.

He leads the way to a counter where he pays and we get fitted with shoes. They look like they're fifty years old and have been worn by literally thousands of bowlers.

He doesn't seem too concerned about the obvious hygiene issue. He takes the shoes and me to a lane. I try to watch the other bowlers to see how they do it.

"I'm gonna fall flat on my face," I tell Billy. "Just warning you."

He only smiles at me. "The point of this is to have fun. It isn't a competition—unless you really are a competitive bowler."

"Are *you* a competitive bowler?" I ask.

He eases in, closes his big, warm hands on either side of my face and kisses me. "Only with people who actually offer me some competition. That won't happen here."

"You're damn right it won't," I mutter.

He couldn't be more delighted with my bad attitude. "Put your shoes on and we'll get started."

We change our shoes. Now I really feel like an old lady.

Billy points to a guy with a beer gut in the lane next to us. "Watch that guy. He has really good technique."

"He isn't in Olympic condition, is he?"

Billy bites back laughter. "Just watch him when he bowls his next ball. The idea is not to let go of the ball until it's already moving at its fastest speed. The momentum of your swing is what sends the ball down the lane. See?"

I nod. The guy in the next lane makes it look easy. He cleans out all the pins twice with both balls.

"Now watch me," Billy tells me.

He goes through the balls on the rack, selects the one he wants, stands back, raises the ball to his eyes, goes deadly serious, and then strides forward. He lowers the ball, swings it back, and releases it.

It soars down the lane in a perfect arc, clears all the pins in a whirl-wind smash, and the ball bangs down behind the lane.

"You didn't tell me you were so good!" I protest. "You tricked me!"

"This is supposed to be fun. Would you feel better if we didn't keep score?"

"What about that?" I point at an electronic scoreboard above the lanes. It lists the number of pins Billy just cleared.

"Don't look at it," he tells me.

I turn away and pretend to sulk.

"Don't turn it into a competition when it isn't one," he tells me. "Just enjoy yourself. Hey, if we grow old together, you just might get good enough to beat me."

I glance over at him. Maybe....

It would be worth fifty years of practice if I did beat him.

He reads my mind. "It all starts right here. Go get your ball and knock 'em dead."

I go over to the rack and select my ball, but when I try to pick it up, I can't even lift it.

"That one is too heavy," Billy tells me.

"No shit, Sherlock," I fire back.

He tries to hold back laughter and fails. "Try this one."

He takes down a neon pink ball. It's much lighter than the first one. I can actually hold this without breaking my arm.

I take it back to the lane, stick my fingers in the holes, and stand back to eye the pins in front of me. I take five rapid paces forward, swing the ball back, and then bring it forward to release it.

I don't let go in time. The ball keeps going and my fingers get stuck in the holes. The momentum of my swing carries the ball up and forward. It weighs so much that it yanks me off my feet.

I go sailing into the lane, fall sideways onto my ass, and the ball slams down on the wooden boards with a thump. Everyone in the whole bowling alley turns around to stare at me.

Billy actually does burst out laughing and rushes over to help me. "That's okay!" he insists. "Nothing to worry about. You're doing great. Just try again. Come on. Are you all right? Did you hurt yourself?"

"Like you care," I mutter.

He can't stop laughing, but I can see he's trying his best not to. I must have looked really ridiculous.

My fingers ache, but at least I can still move them. He picks me up, straightens me out, and rubs my arms and shoulders like I'm a boxer and he's my trainer or something.

He keeps breaking out in snickers. "Don't worry. The same thing happened to me my first time."

"I don't believe you," I snarl.

He laughs again. "Come on. Try again."

I have to shake the kinks out of my arm while I wait for my ball to come back. Some kind of machine spits it out along with a bunch of other balls.

I dread picking it up and making an idiot of myself a second time, but what the hell else am I going to do?

The pins still stand at the end of the lane waiting for me. My disastrous first attempt didn't even touch them.

I position the ball in the same place at my shoulder. This time, I make sure to pay enough attention to how I stick my fingers in the holes. I have to be able to get my fingers out in time to release the ball.

I take my swing, and this time, I actually send the ball down the lane without going there myself.

The ball goes straight into the gutter and doesn't touch the pins that time, either.

"Great!" Billy crows. "Outstanding! You see? You're getting the hang of it."

I point up at the scoreboard. "*That* doesn't say I'm getting the hang of it."

He only beams at me. "I have an idea. How about you bowl all the frames?"

I frown at him. "What does that mean?"

"You can take my turns as well as your own. I won't play. We'll call this a teaching exercise while you get the hang of it. Then you won't see it as competing against me."

I blink at him. "Really?"

"Sure. You're right. Us playing against each other would hardly be fair."

"But sitting there watching me will hardly be any fun for you.

He blushes and grins. "Watching you will be the most fun for me. I can take one for the team."

"Um....thanks."

He nods toward the ball machine. "So it's your turn again."

He sits down and I pick up my ball.

Knowing he's sitting there watching my every move makes me self-conscious, but I don't mind. His gesture of sitting out the game means a lot.

He might be checking out my ass from back there. He might just be fantasizing about what we're going to do back at his place, but I also know he cares. He cares enough to stop playing so I feel more comfortable.

I bowl one more ball before he steps back over to me. "Let me give you some pointers. Come over here."

He takes me back to the same place and gives me a detailed explanation of how and where to release the ball and how to add spin to make it curve into the pins at exactly the right time. On my next shot, I hit all but four pins.

He bursts out in cheers, whistles, and yells, "Outstanding!" as soon as the pins stop flying. I turn around and blush at him.

I bowl three more balls. I don't always knock down any pins. I throw another gutter ball on my last attempt.

He comes over to me, cradles my face in his hands, and gazes deep into my eyes. "You're doing great. Just try to relax. Tonight is your first time ever doing this. You're learning. Don't get down on yourself."

"Yes, Obi-wan," I grumble.

He only smiles and kisses me. "Keep going. You're doing great."

He turns away to go sit down....and we both freeze when we see Danny Brewer in the lane behind us. He's looking straight at us. The knowing flick of his eyes from Billy to me and back again tells me Danny definitely saw Billy kissing me.

It takes me a second realize Danny is here with a bunch of kids—his stepson, Zeke Montgomery, John's daughter, Oakleigh, Felix and Ainsley Santiago, and four other firehouse kids. They're all setting up to bowl.

Danny nods at Billy. "Hey."

"You did not just see that," Billy growls.

A slight smile tugs the corners of Danny's lips, but he doesn't actually smile. "I definitely saw it and it's nice to see. I always thought you two would wind up together. It's about time. You two are good together."

He turns away to deal with the kids. He doesn't say anything else to us. He has his hands full getting them all to sit down and change their shoes.

Billy turns back to me. "Well, it looks like the cat is out of the bag."

"I guess it could be worse. I guess I don't have a problem with everyone at the firehouse finding out."

"I guess not." The cloud lifts from Billy's face and he smiles at me. "At least we don't have to hide it anymore."

He heads back to the bench to sit down, but I grab him to hold him back. "Would you mind....if I take a break? My shoulder is killing me."

He laughs again. "Sure. Let's get a pizza."

We take off our shoes and he orders a pizza from the bowling alley concession stand. We leave the lanes and get a booth away from the noise.

We start eating, but he won't stop staring at me across the table. He doesn't laugh, but he smiles in ways I've never seen before. He looks unimaginably happy—happier than I've ever seen him before.

I eat two slices. He eats four before, out of nowhere, he slides his hand across the table to take mine. He holds it and we keep gazing at each other while we chew.

This is somehow the most romantic date I've ever been on and it isn't even awkward or uncomfortable. It's better than I thought it could be.

We don't say much after that, but this is all just so nice that I don't mind the silence. It's even better than our usual casual banter.

We hold hands on the drive home and he opens the passenger door for me to get out. Our hands slip into each other as if they were made that way.

We go inside and he puts his keys on the kitchen counter. This is all so domestic.

It's almost like I've been living here all along. We could just go into the bedroom, take our clothes off, and crash. We don't have to do anything. Our lives are coming together in a seamless union that just feels right.

Billy pulls off his leather jacket. I should have thought to pack my uniform for work tomorrow. I'll probably spend the night here. Bringing my uniform with me would save me the time of driving to my apartment to change in the morning.

Billy comes over to me, kisses me, and takes my hand before he leads me into the bedroom. He doesn't attack me or tear my clothes off. He sits on the edge of the bed and starts untying his sneakers.

I don't know what to do so I start untying my crop top. His eyes shoot up and he watches me.

We both watch each other get undressed and he pulls down the covers. I walk around the other side of the bed to get in. He bursts into a smirk as we both slide between the sheets.

We scoot toward each other and lock into a deep, warm embrace that wipes away all care. I don't have to worry about what we are or where this is going or anything else. This feels unbelievable.

He kisses my hair and heaves a massive sigh. I feel the same way. His chest gives me the perfect refuge from the whole world. I don't need anything else.

He raises his hand and runs his fingers through my hair.....again .....and again. That slow, soft touch soothes me into a trance. This is exactly where I need to be.

Chapter 18: Brooke

The rescue truck bounces out of the firehouse with the siren wailing. "House on fire—4565 Nightingale Terrace!" Billy yells over the noise. "The neighbor who called it in says the house is home to a family of five—parents and three kids. No word on casualties!"

"They got my order wrong again!" Ellis hollers from the back. "I said no one trapped inside!"

"We don't know they're trapped inside!" Danny tells him. "They could be standing on the sidewalk like the last bunch."

Ellis pretends to frown. "They better be."

Josh turns to me from the seat next to mine. We're working together on the rescue truck today. "I went in first last time. You go first this time, okay?"

I nod. "Yep."

I have to pay attention to putting on my helmet, straightening out my SCBA, and gathering the jump kit and drug box. If I'm going first into a burning house, I need to be ready.

The truck pulls up in front of the house and the Police meet us there. "Any word on the family?!" Keith calls to the officer who directs us where to park.

"The house has two wings branching out to the sides—there and there." The officer points. "The fire is in the main living area between them. The neighbors say the family's bedrooms are in that wing there. No one has come out, so they may be cut off from any exit."

"Got it." Keith turns to us. "Split up. Brooke, Billy, Caleb, and Danny—take that wing over there. Caleb, Ellis, and Josh—come with me to check the other one. We'll meet back here with any casualties."

We all suit up in our SCBAs and protective gear. I leave the drug box and jump kit behind. If the family is trapped in there, we won't be doing any medical work on them. We'll all have to work together to get everyone out alive before we even assess their injuries.

The four of us circle the house, but for some reason, it doesn't have any alternate exits. That's a major design flaw. The only exits are through the main living area which is already engulfed in flames.

The ladder truck shows up a second later and the second crew starts hosing down the fire, but they won't be able to get it under control in time.

"I'm breaking a window!" Billy yells through his mask.

Danny nods. Billy uses his axe to smash the window and we all climb inside.

We enter a deserted child's bedroom with colorful paintings on the walls, shelves of toys on one side, and a mobile of toy airplanes suspended over a tiny bed.

"Break up and search all the rooms!" Danny tells us.

We separate. This house has four bedrooms in this wing alone. Billy, Caleb, and Danny go check the other children's rooms.

I go into the master bedroom and find three little boys huddled on the floor by the bed. Their mother sprawls on the floor grimacing and writhing in pain.

The boys range in age from a sober-looking eight-year-old, a freckle-faced five-year-old, and a four-year-old who keeps whimpering in terror.

The eight-year-old holds the youngest with both arms wrapped around him.

The boys crowd around their mother shooting terrified glances at me and then toward the door. They must realize by now that the house is on fire and they have no way out.

I see them looking up at me like I'm a monster or something. I tear off my mask. I shouldn't, but I need to calm them down and show them I'm a person.

"It's all right," I breathe. "My name is Brooke and I'm a paramedic with the fire department. We're here to get all of you out of the house. Can you tell me what's wrong with your mom?"

"She got hurt," the oldest tells me in a voice that is way too serious for his age.

I can see that she got hurt. The fact that he doesn't tell me means the cause is something I don't want to think about.

"We're gonna help her," I tell him. "We're going to help all of you. What are your names?"

"I'm Dion," the oldest tells me. "This is Finn and this is Georgie." He indicates his middle brother and then the youngest.

"What's your mom's name?" I ask.

"Sadie," Dion replies and little Georgie bursts into tears.

"It's all right, sweetie," I tell him. "We're gonna get you out and take your mom to the hospital. Come on. I'll help you."

I'm about to pick him up when Billy and the other guys show up. "Take your masks off," I tell them and turn back to the boys. "These are firefighters from Howe Firehouse. We're gonna get you out." I turn back to Billy. "It looks like the mother has broken ribs. Could you carry her out?"

"Sure. No problem."

He moves in to pick her up. The boys don't get out of the way.

"This is Billy," I tell them. "He's gonna help your mom. We'll carry you all out of the house, okay?"

I pick up Georgie, but he fights me and tries to get back to his mother. "Mommy!!" he shrieks. "Mommy!!"

Caleb tries to pick up Dion, but the boy shrugs Caleb off. "Let me take him," Dion tells us. "I'll take care of him."

I let go of Georgie. Dion wraps his arms around his brother and steers him out of the way.

Things get easier when Billy picks up the mother. Danny picks up Finn.

I plan to steer the boys back to what must be Georgie's room, but the fire has already started moving down the hall.

"Break the window, Caleb," I tell him. We can get out this way."

"You bet," he replies.

He takes his axe to the master bedroom windows. They're much bigger and extend closer to the floor. From there, we can step right down onto the front lawn.

He smashes out the whole window all the way down to the floor. Billy carries Sadie out first and takes off across the grass to the waiting ambulance.

Josh meets us there and Billy lowers Sadie onto the gurney. "You'll be all right here," he murmurs to her. "The paramedics will check you out and take you to the hospital." He turns to Josh. "Her name is Sadie. Brooke said she has broken ribs."

Billy tries to pull away, but Sadie clutches at his hands. She peers up at him with huge eyes brimming with emotion. "Thank you so much!" she chokes. Her eyes dart to me. "Thank you all so much!"

"Try to relax, Ma'am," I tell her. "We need to check out all four of you."

Danny brings the boys over to sit on the ambulance's back bumper. He kneels down in front of Dion. "Did any of you breathe the smoke?"

Dion shakes his head. "We woke up and saw the flames. We went into my mom's room and found her on the floor. We didn't know what to do, so we just stayed there."

Josh and I bend over Sadie. I put her on oxygen and hand her a pillow. "Hold this against your ribs. It will stabilize the fractures so you can breathe better. Did you lose consciousness at any time?"

I check her pupils, but they're fine.

Josh gets in Sadie's face. "I'm going to do a physical examination of your body, Ma'am. I need to assess if you have any other injuries. Are you okay if I do that?"

She nods and sinks back on the gurney while I take her vital signs.

Josh starts checking her head, neck, shoulders, arms, and then very gently feeling around her ribs. "Is this the only spot that hurts, Ma'am?" he asks. "Do you have any pain anywhere else?"

She shakes her head.

I'm just taking the BP cuff off her arm. Josh works his way down to her pelvis. "Any pain here, Ma'am?"

At that moment, a car screeches up to the curb. It can't get any closer with two firetrucks and two ambulances already parked there.

I don't pay much attention until the driver jumps out, leaves his engine running, and storms over to the ambulance.

The cops try to get in his path to stop him, but he straight-arms right through them and barges over to us.

He snatches Josh by the shoulder of his shirt and yanks him away from the patient. "Get your filthy hands off my wife!" the guy thunders. "Touch her again and I'll kill you!"

The minute he opens his mouth, a powerful stench of booze, cigarettes, and something else blasts me in the face. All his movements are way too big and clumsy. He's out of his mind drunk.

I try to step in. "Sir, if you don't mind, my partner was just...."

The guy clubs me out of the way and rushes the gurney trying to get to Sadie.

The three boys react in a heartbeat, rocket off the ambulance bumper, and try to get to the gurney, too. "Mom!" Dion yells.

Georgie immediately starts screeching, "Mommy! Mommy!" again and stretching his arms to try to get to his mother. Only the fire crew personnel standing around stop him.

Danny manages to wrap his arms around all three boys to keep them out of danger. The man—Sadie's husband—is so infuriated that he barely sees anyone in front of him.

He bends over the gurney and starts fumbling with the straps holding her onto it. "You're coming with me right now!" he bellows. "You're coming with me right now! Get up!"

Billy steps in, plants his big body between the guy and Sadie, and uses his bulk to block the guy from getting near her. "Your wife is injured, dude. This guy is a paramedic. He was checking her out. That's all. Now back away so they can take her to the hospital."

"Get the hell out of my way!" the guy roars. "How dare you keep her from me! I'll kill you! I'll kill you all!"

The guy throws a punch so fast that no one can stop him. He decks Billy right in the eye.

Billy's head whips sideways and he goes ballistic. None of us have a chance to say or do anything before he bellows right back at the guy, lunges for him, crushes the guy's arms to his sides, and tackles him flat on the ground.

Billy keeps roaring in fury while he uses all his weight to pin the guy down and hold him there. The husband thrashes, kicks, and yells curses at everyone, especially Josh. The guy seems more murderously vengeful against Josh for touching Sadie than the husband is against Billy for restraining him.

The cops swarm in and surround both men. I lose sight of them in the scuffle, and a second later, the cops haul the husband away in handcuffs.

Billy gets to his feet. John, Keith, and Caleb go over to him. "You okay?" John asks. "Sit down and let Sophie take a look at your eye."

Billy swipes John's hand away, but Billy stops himself from actually touching John. That would be a major infraction, but Billy doesn't do it.

He spins the other way. "I don't need anyone checking me out. Just leave me alone."

He stalks off toward the ladder truck and starts helping the second crew hose down the fire. He doesn't come back.

John, Keith, and Caleb stare after him. None of them goes to bring him back.

Danny is having a hard time calming the boys down. They all scream for their mother. They don't calm down until he actually lets them come over to the gurney to be near her.

"You see?" he tells them. "She's all right. Your father is gone. We're going to take her to the hospital now. You can ride with her. You can stay with her the whole time. Come on. Get in."

That's the cue for me and Josh to finish checking out Sadie and load her into the ambulance. The boys cooperate a lot more once we get her inside.

Danny comes with us. Josh and I are both too busy working on Sadie to deal with the boys, but at least they aren't injured. They're just obviously petrified—of their own father. This is not good.

Drew and Ellis shut the ambulance doors with all of us on board. The last sight I catch of Billy is of him across the lawn helping the other firefighters with their hoses. He doesn't even look when Ellis shuts the doors and Drew drives us off into the night.

Chapter 19: Billy

I throw my duffel bag into my locker extra hard and slam the door. I can't stop fuming about that call.

I don't care about the bruise to the side of my face or the swelling around my eye. That will go away. I don't even care that the guy hit me before he got arrested.

I'm just about to go out to the garage to start my shift when Brooke walks in. I see her out of the corner of my eye so I don't look up.

She comes over to me. "Hey!" she murmurs. "You okay?"

"I'm fine," I lie without looking up. "I couldn't be better."

"Do you want to talk about it?" she asks.

"NO!!" I yell out before I think to stop myself and turn away from her. I go over to the bulletin board and pretend to read it. I don't want to talk to anyone, but I have to start my shift.

She follows me, but she doesn't get upset by my attitude. "If you change your mind, I'm always here to listen."

"I just hate guys like that." I try to bite off the words. I promised myself I wouldn't talk about it, but the words come out in spite of my best efforts to hold them back.

"I get it," she murmurs. "He was a monster. We all saw how scared the kids were."

"He's supposed to protect them," I snarl. "He's supposed to protect all of them."

"I know. You protected all of us—the whole crew. You defended Josh." She puts out her hand to touch my arm. "You're one of the good guys."

"No, I'm not!" I swing at her to stop her from touching me, but I pull it in time so I don't actually knock her hand away.

I can't stand being around her, so I walk out into the garage. The rest of the crew is already out there talking. She won't try to talk to me around them—not in any serious way.

I walk right over to them. "Hey, slugger!" Keith greets me.

"I'm not the slugger," I point out. "I'm the sluggee."

The others laugh. "You brought that sucker down like an MMA champ," Danny points out. "That was a beautiful sight to see."

"At least the cocksucker is in jail now," I mutter.

Josh claps me on the shoulder. "Thank you for stepping in the way you did. You saved us all a big headache."

"And got one for myself," I point out.

More people laugh. I'm just starting to hope this shift goes a little better than yesterday's. I can almost forget that Brooke is here.

She won't be fooled by me joking around with the rest of the crew. I'm going to have to work a lot harder to avoid her.

I'm just about to make another joke about that call when a hush falls over the group. "Look, man," Danny whispers.

I follow his eyes. He glances past my shoulder and my stomach drops when two cop cars pull up in the firehouse driveway.

They block the doors so the trucks won't be able to get out, but no one mentions that.

Police Chief Jim Walker and Detective Eli Hill get out of one car along with two other plain-clothes detectives. Four uniformed officers get out of the other car.

Chief Walker and Detective Hill stop in front of us. "Howdy folks," Chief Walker begins. "We need to take statements from all of you about yesterday's incident."

"What do you need our statements for?" Keith rumbles. "You were all there. You saw what happened."

"Eli and I weren't," Chief Walker replies, "but this is just by the book. We need statements from everyone."

"Shouldn't you be talking to John about this first?" Chris asks.

Chief Walker opens his mouth to answer, but just then, John comes downstairs from his office.

He shakes Chief Walker's hand. "You came over quick. I didn't have time to tell the crew you were coming."

"Why are we being questioned?" Danny asks again. All we did was protect our patients and Billy restrained a violent drunk so your boys could arrest him. None of us did anything wrong."

"And don't even think about finding any fault with what Billy did," Brooke chimes in. "That asshole struck first."

"We know all that and we aren't here to find fault with anything anybody did," Chief Walker replies. "We have fourteen other witnesses from the Police force alone who all saw the incident. Even if we didn't, the dash cam on the second ambulance caught the whole thing. We just need your statements to add to the mountain of evidence we need to put this guy away."

"How can you put him away?" Josh asks. "All he did was punch Billy. That's a misdemeanor assault charge."

"We have evidence that he also assaulted his wife and broke her ribs before he set fire to the house with her and the three boys inside it," Chief Walker replies.

Gasps go around the group. "Jesus!" Ellis murmurs.

"I thought I smelled something like gas when he showed up at the scene," Brooke remarks. "It was kinda hard to tell because he was so tanked on booze, but it was still there."

"Exactly," Chief Walker replies. "We tested his clothes and took chemical analysis samples from his skin when we booked him. He had gas on his clothes and hands—which was the accelerant that started the fire."

"That is some messed up shit—setting fire to your own house with your wife and children inside," Caleb murmurs. "A guy like that shouldn't be walking around on the street."

"That's why we need as much evidence as possible to put him away." Chief Walker turns to Brooke. "You can include in your statement that you smelled gas on him when he tried to interfere with your work. Billy, you can go with Eli here."

I stiffen. I don't want to go anywhere with any cop to answer questions about anything, but I don't really have a choice. John stands guard over all of us just to make sure we do it.

The other officers divide up the crew. I try not to pay attention to Chief Walker interviewing Brooke.

I appreciate her standing up for me. I appreciate everyone standing up for me, but that doesn't make this any easier.

Will she tell Chief Walker that we were in a relationship and that's the reason I stepped in to stop that idiot from going near her?

I have to get my head screwed on straight when Detective Hill leads me across the garage to the opposite wall. He takes out his tablet and starts tapping on it.

"So can you tell me when you first realized the offender was trying to interfere with Mrs. Monroe's medical care?" he asks.

I shrug and wind up squirming. "I didn't have to realize 'cuz I was standing right there the whole time. Brooke found her and the boys in the house and the woman couldn't walk on her own. Brooke asked me to carry the woman out of the house, so I was the one who put her on the gurney. I was still standing there when Josh started examining her. I didn't have a chance to leave before the dude showed up and started throwing accusations at Josh."

"So did Mr. Monroe make accusations against you for carrying his wife?"

"He couldn't because he didn't see me carrying her. I had already put her down by the time he showed up. He only cared about Josh."

"Why did he hit you, then?" Detective Hill asks.

"Because I stepped between him and the patient. He pulled Josh away from her and then Brooke tried to intervene." I bristle. "I never did anything to that woman. All I did was try to help her. No one can say I did anything inappropriate."

"No one is saying that," he replies.

"Are you sure? Is that jackass accusing me of doing something with her?"

Now it's his turn to squirm. "He's saying a lot of things that are completely stupid and we all know they're lies."

"So he *is* accusing me of doing something."

"Listen, man," he tells me. "He's making accusations against everyone—including people who were either on the opposite side of the scene or weren't there at all. If you ask me, he was so stinking drunk he doesn't even remember what he did. He's even making accusations against Chief Brewer, so consider yourself in good company. His accusations don't mean anything—and you saw yourself that he accused

Josh for nothing. Don't take it personally. Now let's get back to your statement."

I shift my weight a few more times, but he's right. If this moron is making accusations against John, then the dipshit really must be out of his mind. John was nowhere near the ambulances or the incident or the patient at the time.

Detective Hill checks his tablet again. "So when you tackled the offender, did you try to hit him?"

"I wanted to, but I was too busy holding him down. He's stronger than he looks."

He looks up at me. "You wanted to, though."

"Of course I wanted to. I wanted to pound him into the dirt for hitting me."

A slight smile tugs the corners of Detective Hill's lips, but he holds it back. "Had you ever met Carson Monroe or his wife Sadie before that day?"

I raise my eyebrows. "Carson....Monroe? That's his name? Of course I never met him before that night. I never knew his name until right now."

He nods and finishes tapping on his device. "Okay, man. That will be all we need for now, but I need you to make yourself available for further questioning if we need it. Okay?"

I'm glaring at him too badly to answer. How am I the one getting questioned by the Police when I'm the injured party here?

He sees me shooting him a death glare and he really does smile before he walks away. He rejoins the rest of the group where Chief Walker and the other officers are talking to John and the crew.

I can't go over there. I can't go anywhere near them. I wouldn't be able to go over there even if Brooke wasn't there—which she is.

I storm out of the garage without looking back. I won't be able to stay gone because I'm in the middle of a shift, but I need to cool down.

Just don't ask me how I'm going to do that with this on my shoulders.

Chapter 20: Billy

I ease into John's office, but I hesitate to go near his desk. Quarterly performance reviews are the bane of my existence—only slightly less excruciating than giving incident reports.

John doesn't notice my discomfort—or maybe he does. He goes through the same process four times a year—sometimes more.

He waves at the chairs opposite his desk. "Take a seat, man."

He says it casually. He always keeps it casual, but that doesn't make this any easier. Nothing can.

I can't think of anything worse than getting called up in front of the Fire Chief to have my job performance scrutinized, criticized, evaluated, and measured to see if I'm cutting the mustard.

I drag my sad ass over to the chair, but I can't stop squirming. I hate this. I really wish I could quit the fire service so I didn't have to go through this, but I can't quit. This job is everything to me.

He leans back in his chair and studies me across his desk. "So how's it going, man?" he asks.

I shrug at nothing. "It's going."

"I'm putting you in for a commendation for restraining that guy at the scene yesterday," he tells me.

My head shoots up. "You what?"

"You put the safety of a patient and your crew above your own. You took a hit and still managed to restrain the guy until the Police got to him. You did great."

I look away. If I did so great, why am I getting questioned by the Police?

I don't say that out loud, though. I don't want a commendation for that. I just want everyone to forget it, but they won't. They'll keep beating the dead horse for the rest of eternity.

John checks his computer. "I want to talk about why you've been so touchy lately. You obviously have something on your mind."

"It's none of your business if I do," I snarl.

I shouldn't talk to him like this, but I do it anyway. He would be the last person on God's green Earth I would ever talk to about this—or anything else for that matter.

He reads my mind. "Whatever is on your mind isn't my business, but your job performance is—and part of your job performance is how well you get along and communicate with your crewmates."

"Who says I don't get along and communicate with my crew-mates?" I demand.

He spreads both hands. "Now you're going out of your way to make this as difficult as possible. We aren't stupid, Billy. We can all see and feel you storming around the place simmering away like a volcano ready to blow. I only bring it up because we all care enough to want to help you. You don't have to tell me what's bothering you, but you either need to deal with it or talk to someone else. You can't just keep fuming and blowing up at people for trying to talk to you."

I look away again. I hate the fact that he's right. I do need to talk to someone. I just can't think of who I would talk to.

He changes his tone and lowers his voice. He actually sounds soft right now—not like my boss but like a good man who actually cares enough to help a friend.

"Whatever it is, you can tell us," he murmurs. "We're your friends. We're family. You know that. You know every person here has your back no matter what it is."

I can't look at him. "Do you ever feel like......do you ever feel like no one around here knows who you really are?" I glance over at him. "Of course you don't because everyone knows who you really are and everyone loves you. You wouldn't understand."

He stares at me in horror. "What the hell is going on with you, man? That incident yesterday was nothing. It means nothing. You handled it perfectly. You have no reason to think anyone would criticize what you did."

I clamp my mouth shut to stop myself from saying anything else. None of these people has a flippin' clue—and they never will because I would never tell them why the incident does mean something. It means a lot. It means everything.

He glances at his computer again. "Why don't you talk to Brooke about it?" he suggests.

"Forget it," I snap. "No way."

He looks up. "Why not? You two are good for each other."

"Not anymore."

His eyes fall out of their sockets. "Why not? Did something happen? Your relationship was going so good...."

"We don't have a relationship," I interrupt. "Not anymore."

His jaw drops in horror. He barely speaks above a whisper. "What the hell happened?"

I shift in my seat again. Brooke is the last thing in the world I want to talk to John about, especially at my quarterly performance review.

"So are you going to give me a bad performance review because of my relationship with Brooke? Is that it?"

I hear myself being extra harsh on him. I hate myself for reacting like this.

I should confide in him. I should tell him everything. I trust him more than any other man alive—and he's right. I know he cares and I know he'd have my back. He would support me no matter what—but I can't tell him. I can never tell anyone.

He shuts his mouth in a big hurry. His face goes dark, but he doesn't pull the old Boss routine on me. He's too good for that.

"Your performance—and your reviews—depend on you getting along with your crewmates. Your performance and your reviews depend on you not making the firehouse a tense, uncomfortable minefield that could blow up in our faces at any moment."

"I'm not doing that," I counter. "My personal life is no one's business as long as it doesn't interfere with me doing my job."

"Then make sure it doesn't interfere," he tells me.

I give him one nod. That's all I can muster right now.

"You can go, Billy," he tells me. "Keep up the good work."

I get out of there as quick as I can and go back downstairs.

He's right about something else. I need to make sure my personal life doesn't interfere with the job.

Everything was going perfect until all this stuff started up with Brooke. My personal life never interfered before because I never had a personal life.

That was my mistake—getting involved with her. I knew it was a bad call when I did it. Now I just have to correct that mistake. Then everything will go back to the way it was before.

I don't want to talk to anyone, so I pretend to check the bulletin board. I don't expect to find anything I don't already know about.

I experience a whole new wave of agony when I see a big circle on the schedule and a bunch of arrows pointing to tomorrow's shift. Someone has written inside the circle, *Leila & Leon visit.*

I stand there staring as the bottom drops out from under my world. I can't think straight.

I tear myself away and go into the locker room. I'd like to shut the door, but that would only draw attention to me—attention I don't want.

I pull out my phone and call Vince Jaeger. He's on the overnight shift tonight.

"Hey, man!" he greets me.

"Hey, pal. Would you mind switching shifts with me tomorrow? I'll work for you on Friday night if you cover for me tomorrow. Help a brother out."

"Sure, dude. No problem," he tells me. "What's the occasion?"

"No occasion. I just want to switch. Thanks a lot. I appreciate it."

I hang up as politely as I can, but when I turn around to leave the locker room, I stop in my tracks when I see Brooke standing there.

I want to run from her, but I can't. There's nowhere to run because we work together all the time. This is a nightmare. It's worse than a nightmare. It's a catastrophe.

She steps into the locker room. The tension between us escalates to the breaking point.

"Why are you switching shifts tomorrow?" she asks me. "You'll miss Leila's visit."

"I don't need to see Leila. I know what she looks like and I know what babies look like."

I try to turn away from her, but her presence somehow rivets me to the floor. I should walk out of the locker room right now—now that she isn't blocking the only exit.

Something stops me from doing that. She holds some power over me that I don't understand.

She takes another step and my skin crawls. I can't stand her this close to me, but I can't leave, either—much as I want to.

She watches me writhe in my own skin. "Billy?" she chokes.

The sound of her voice tears me in half. She sounds so broken and crushed. I did that to her. I hurt her like that. Christ, I'm such a waste of human flesh. I can't even love a good woman who wants me.

"So.....is it all over between us?" Her voice breaks. Is she crying right now? I'll never know because I can't look at her.

I can't even answer that question. I can't lose her....and yet I've already lost her. I lost her by being a loser and an animal.

I made the worst mistake of my life by thinking I could have her. She's too good for me. I knew that. I just fooled myself that it could ever work out between us when it couldn't.

She takes one more step toward me and says, "Billy....."

She lays her hand on my arm. That touch blows my head apart. I can't stand her touching me—not ever again.

I shake off her hand. I try to do it gently, but I might even fail at that, too.

This nest of snakes in my guts won't leave me alone. I have no choice but to leave the room and put as much distance between me and her as I can.

I go through the rest of my shift without going near her, talking to her, and avoiding all eye contact with her.

I can play it off around the others. I can just act like nothing is bothering me. I can't do that with her.

We all go upstairs to the breakroom for lunch. Brooke isn't there, and a minute later, Sophie comes over to me.

"Brooke is downstairs in the locker room crying," Sophie murmurs under her breath.

"So?" I fire back.

"Aren't you going to talk to her? Aren't you at least going to find out what's bothering her?"

"No," I reply and walk away. I already know what's bothering Brooke.

Talking to her will only make her more upset and I can't risk losing it myself—which is exactly what would happen if I ever let myself be in the same room with her again.

Chapter 21: Billy

I show up for my shift on Friday. I successfully avoided the Leila and Leon visit.

I've spent the last three days listening to everyone gush about how wonderful Leon is and how good Leila looks and how happy she and Keith are. Spectacular. How long will it take for everyone to forget about that, too?

No one makes any fuss about me starting the shift in Vince's place. Brooke isn't working today, thank the stars. I don't have to worry about avoiding her.

Things are slowly getting back to the way they were before. Word must be spreading through the grapevine that Brooke and I are over. No one mentions us avoiding each other.

We still work together on calls, but that doesn't make it any less awkward.

Things will smooth out in time. I just have to put this behind me and go back to my old life alone. I liked it that way and it worked. I can do it again.

I get started on the truck checks. Jessie Nash and Sophie McNish are our paramedics on the rescue truck today. Keith isn't working so that makes Danny our ranking firefighter.

He shows up and we work together to finish the checklist. We get halfway through it when we get a callout.

Keith isn't here so I hop in the driver's seat. I shoot Danny a grin on the side. "Don't think you're going to fight me for it. I'll whoop your ass."

He only laughs and buckles into the passenger seat where I usually sit. "I don't want to drive. I'll just sit here and tell you what to do."

"Just do it nicely," I tell him. "Don't hurt my sensitive feelings."

He laughs again. I make sure the two paramedics and Ellis, Caleb, and Theo Gough are all sitting down with the doors closed.

I hit the lights and sirens and pull out onto the road. "Another motor vehicle wreck on the highway!" Danny reads from the computer. "Four patients."

"I want to see the manager!" Ellis yells and we all laugh.

We stop laughing when we get to the scene. A single passenger car sits on its roof against the retaining wall. Most of the roof and one side have been completely smashed in.

Danny and Theo get busy blocking the car to stabilize it. I have to get down on my hands and knees to peer through the passenger window at the patients inside.

I freeze when I see Sadie Monroe and her three little boys trapped in the car. Little Georgie has fallen out of his car seat and huddles in a ball on the smashed roof which is now acting as the floor.

Dion, the oldest boy, keeps fighting to get out of his seatbelt, but it's jammed. It traps him under the most crumpled part of the roof. He has to hunch over just to fit under there.

Finn has unbuckled himself and crouches next to Dion's seat. Finn yanks at the seatbelt trying to get it out of the buckle.

"Hey!" I greet them all. "Remember me? I'm Billy. Remember—from the house? Come on. We're gonna get you out."

"HE'S OUT THERE!!" Sadie screeches in my face. "HE'S OUT THERE!! HE DROVE US OFF THE ROAD!!"

I glance over at her. I don't think she's trapped, but she's out of her mind hysterical about something.

I don't have to think too hard to figure out who she's talking about. Josh hit the nail on the head. Her husband punching me was just a misdemeanor assault. The Police wouldn't be able to hold him for that.

I concentrate on the task at hand. Jessie comes over to me. "How bad are their injuries?"

"I don't see any. Go around the other side and check the driver while I get the boys out."

She leaves to help the mother. I crawl halfway through the window and use my extrication tool to slice through Dion's seatbelt. "Come on, buddy. I'm getting you out. Come on."

He climbs into my arms and I pull him out of the car. The minute he gets out, he attacks me trying to fight his way back inside. "Get my brother! Get my brother!"

"I am getting him, buddy," I tell him. "Give me a second."

I crawl back inside and pick up Georgie. He thrashes in my arms and tries to get to his mother. "Mommy! Mommy!" he yells.

She keeps screaming again and again, "HE'S OUT THERE!! HE'S OUT THERE!!" At least she's screaming at Jessie now instead of me.

Jessie tries to talk to the mother through the smashed driver's window. The woman doesn't see her son trying to get to her.

I can't wait any longer. I gotta get these kids out of the car. I lift Georgie off his feet and try as gently as I can to restrain him while I take him out through the broken passenger window. That leaves one boy left.

I stand Georgie on the pavement in front of Dion. Georgie tries to lunge back to the window to get to his mother, but Dion comes to my rescue.

He grabs his little brother and holds onto Georgie talking fast into the little boy's ear. "It's all right, Georgie," Dion tells him. "The firemen will get Mommy out of the car. Just stay here. I'll take care of you."

I make sure Dion has a firm grip on Georgie before I turn back to the window to get Finn.

Before I can bend over a third time, the high-pitched squeal of screeching tires echoes out of the distance. That sound shatters the noise and makes me look up—almost as if I knew what was about to happen.

Sadie gives an ear-splitting scream and starts trying to fight her way out of the car, but she can't do that when the whole vehicle is already a crumpled mass of twisted iron.

Dion and Georgie both turn back the other way to look, too. Time stands still when another car blasts through the Police barricade coming straight for us. It's coming way too fast.

I spot the boys' father through the windshield. He glares at all of us and clenches his fists on the wheel. He compresses his lips and revs the motor to charge us in his car.

I dive for Dion and Georgie, but I already know it's too late. The two boys stand with their backs to me. Dion rests his hands on Georgie's shoulders to keep his little brother close to him.

I grab both of them and spin the other way to cover them with my body, but the car gets to us before I can do anything.

I barely get the boys behind me when the car smashes into me from behind. I close my arms around Dion as tightly as I can, but the impact tears Georgie away.

I feel myself flying across the road. I curl into a ball to protect Dion. He's all I have left. I might not be able to save myself, but at least I can protect him.

I curl my body around him and slam down on the pavement. I feel myself tumbling over and over and over again. Dion screams in my arms. I might be hurting him by holding onto him so tightly, but I can't let go.

I roll for a long way and hit something hard before I collapse on the ground. Everything hurts. I don't dare to open my eyes to find out how bad it is.

Dion huddles against me and doesn't move. Please Dear God don't let anything have happened to him. I couldn't live with that.

I'm still lying there when Jessie bends over me. "Billy...." she pants. "Don't move. We have to immobilize you and take you to the hospital. Just....let us check the boy. It's okay, Billy. You can let go now."

I feel her tugging my arms, but I can't loosen them. The part of my brain that unlocks my arms from around Dion doesn't work anymore.

Jessie has to pry my arms off. My world crumbles when they take Dion away from me.

I hear his voice getting farther away. "Billy!! Is he all right? Billy! Don't let him be hurt too bad. I want to stay with Billy."

"Let the paramedics take care of him," Danny tells him. "They'll take him to the hospital. You can't help him now."

I don't open my eyes to watch Danny take Dion away. The pain in my head and body builds to an unbearable agony.

"We're going to board you up now, Billy," Jessie tells me.

"I need to do a physical exam, Billy," Sophie tells me. "Can you handle that? We'll give you some painkillers first."

I can't answer. I have to grit my teeth to hold in all this pain. That jackass ran me down with his car. He could have killed both his children. Who the hell does that shit?

"I'm starting an IV, Billy," Jessie tells me. She pries my arm down and cinches the tourniquet around my bicep.

Caleb, Theo, and Ellis put the cervical collar around my neck and then load me onto a backboard and the gurney. I can't think, but then I get swept into a whole new world of pain when Sophie starts doing the physical examination.

I howl in agony when she touches all my injuries. I don't even want to think about the damage, but I don't feel any broken bones. That's a mercy.

Chapter 22: Brooke

I shuffle my feet in the hospital waiting room. The whole fire crew gathers around waiting to see Billy.

I can't stop knitting my fingers together. My stomach hurts from the tension, but at least I'm not crying over our breakup anymore.

I can't stand all the other women on our crew trying to support me and telling me there might still be a way for me and Billy to work it out. That will never happen now. I don't even know how or why it ended. He never explains anything to me.

Now he's in the hospital. He's a hero for saving Dion's life. John is already talking about decorating Billy for this.

I glance over my shoulder toward the doors leading to the hospital ward. Why am I even here? Billy doesn't want to see me. Me coming will only make him uncomfortable.

I'm part of the fire crew, though, and so is he. I would come to the hospital to support any other member of our crew who got hurt in the line of duty.

If Billy and I are over, then we're back to being crewmates and co-workers—which means me coming to support him in the hospital.

Only pure spite would keep me away. I couldn't do that. Even Ellen and Leila are here.

I didn't tell anyone about Billy changing his shift to avoid seeing Leila. I can't understand why he doesn't want to see her. They've been as close as the rest of the firehouse family.

He wouldn't have gotten hurt at all if he didn't change his shift. Vince would have been on that call instead of Billy.

I can't even think that Vince would have gotten hurt in Billy's place. Billy got hurt saving Dion because Billy knew the family from the fire.

He connected with them when he protected Sadie from her drunk husband. That's why Billy rescued Dion. That's why Carson Monroe ran Billy down with that car.

So many thoughts and feelings war inside me. I don't know what to think or how to think them. This whole situation is so much worse than I ever thought it could be.

Getting serious about Billy and then having it all come crashing down around my ears—that would be bad enough.

He could have gotten killed on that call. Then what would I do?

I can't imagine my life without Billy, but that's exactly the future I'm looking at right now. I'm staring down the barrel of years and decades ahead without the one man I could have been happy with. How can I give that up?

I just have to because he ended it. It's all over. He doesn't want me.

That's not true. I know he wants me. He wants me as much as I want him.

We love each other. I know that now.

I hate myself for not telling him when I had the chance, but I know it's true. I know it in the core of my soul the same way I know he loves me.

Something else is stopping him from living that happy life—the life he most wants, the life he deserves. Something has convinced him he doesn't deserve it. He'll never be happy until he realizes that he does deserve it.

I can't give him that. He has to find it for himself. Until he does, he's no good for me or anyone else. He's better off alone.

I need a man who really wants to be with me—a man who embraces this life together as fully as I do. I can't get involved with someone who isn't all in.

Thinking that doesn't make this any easier, especially not when a nurse comes through the doors and says, "You can come in now."

John, Keith, and Danny go first. The rest of us follow.

I hover near the back of the crowd. I don't want to make it out like I'm in any big rush to see Billy because I'm not.

The nurse leads the way onto the ward and into a private room. The rest of the crew packs inside. I have to wedge myself into the very back corner.

John and the others gather around Billy's bed. Bruises cover his face, run down his neck, and darken his arms where they stick out of his hospital gown. He looks absolutely awful, but at least he's awake.

"How you doing, man?" John tells him. "The doctors say you don't have any broken bones. You just have one monster concussion. You'll be back on the horse in no time."

"I'm all right." Billy glances around at everyone. "Thank you all for coming."

"You're the man, Billy," Danny tells him. "You saved Dion's life. You're a hero."

Billy whips around. "Where is he? Is he okay? Did he get hurt? I tried to protect him. I didn't get to see him before you took him away."

"He's in the hospital, too," John replies. "He keeps asking to see you. He worships you for saving him."

Billy collapses back on the pillow. "I was so worried about him. Are the other boys okay?"

A tense hush falls over the rest of the crew. I've been dreading this moment. I thank Heaven I'm not the one standing by Billy's bed. I wouldn't be able to tell him.

"Sadie and Finn are fine," John murmurs under his breath. "Georgie didn't make it."

Billy clamps his eyes shut. He must have been dreading this moment, too. He must have been lying in his hospital bed worrying about what happened to both boys. Now he knows.

He tries to compress his lips, but emotion tears his features out of position. He throws his arm over his face and breaks down in silent, racking sobs. We can barely hear him gasping for breath in the terrible silence. He doesn't make any other sound.

Tears sting my eyes. Jessie and Sophie start crying, too. The other male firefighters who were at the scene sniff. No one thinks worse of Billy for losing it.

John clamps his hand on Billy's shoulder. "You did everything you could to save him. His father is in jail charged with homicide. The Police want to question you, but it's just a formality. There were too many other witnesses. We'll let you rest. You come back and see me when you're ready to return to work. We're all pulling for you and we're all proud of you. You're a hero, man."

John squeezes Billy's shoulder one more time, but Billy doesn't take his arm down—not until we all leave.

I'm the closest to the door so I leave first. The rest of the crew files back to the waiting room.

"Poor Billy," Danny murmurs.

Sophie wipes tears off her cheeks. "He needs to see Dion. Dion will help Billy deal with it."

"I'll talk to Sadie about bringing Dion to see Billy," John replies. "I know she's already asked to see him."

"So.....do we just leave?" Ellis asks. "That was the shortest hospital visit in history. We should do more."

"Leaving Billy alone is the nicest thing we can do for him," Keith replies. "He won't want us hanging around making a fuss over him."

"You're right," John adds. "We can welcome Billy back to the firehouse when he's ready to come. He'll need our support to get his life back on track."

There's nothing else to say, so we all just drift away. I'm on shift today, so Chris and I load into the rescue truck with Keith, Danny, Ellis, Caleb, and Vince. He's covering Billy's shifts while Billy is in the hospital.

The truck doesn't feel the same without Billy here. I almost don't care anymore if we broke up. I just want him to come back.

I want him to get his life back. If going out with me is that hard for him, then I don't want us to go out with each other. I just want him to be okay. I want him to be happy. He's been through enough.

Chapter 23: Billy

I groan when I swing my legs off my hospital bed and put my feet on the floor. My body feels like trash and looks just as bad.

Dark purple bruises cover my arms and legs, my back and sides, my shoulders, my neck, and my head. It's a damn miracle I didn't break any bones in that accident.

It wasn't an accident. That cocksucker ran me down in his car.

I could live with that if only Georgie was still alive. Not even saving Dion can make up for that.

I want to get murderously, vengefully furious at Carson Monroe for killing Georgie and putting Dion in the hospital—and that's saying nothing about what he did to Sadie and Finn.

I can't even get mad at the son of a bitch. I'm too broken up about Georgie.

I know I did everything to save him, but it doesn't help. Just thinking about him makes me feel like I might start crying again.

I don't care anymore that I broke down in front of the whole fire crew. Every one of them has lost people on calls. They understand how one special patient or victim can affect someone.

I guess Georgie is that for me now—the one patient I couldn't save. I would gladly have died in his place. Now I'm stuck here wishing I was dead.

He'll never grow up. He'll never become a man. He'll never play or laugh or watch TV or do any of the things a boy should do.

His own father took that away from him. I can't live with that, but I have to.

I wince when I turn to the pile of clothes on the bed next to me. Ellen brought them for me so I have something to wear home from the hospital. My uniform was saturated in blood when the crew brought me in. The hospital staff incinerated that uniform long ago.

I wince and pant when I bend over to put on my pants. My back hurts the worst of everything where I rolled on the pavement.

Only one part of my body is uninjured. A perfectly Dion-shaped area of white marks my chest and stomach where I held onto him. I protected him. What a pathetic scrap of comfort that is.

I'm just buttoning my pants and pulling my gown off to put on my shirt when the door opens. Jim Walker and Eli Hill walk in.

"How you doing, Billy?" Chief Walker asks.

"You can see how I'm doing," I growl over my shoulder. "John told me you wanted to question me about the incident."

"If you don't mind. We can do it later if you want to wait."

"No, get it done now. What do you want to know? I'm sure you have plenty of other witnesses to what happened."

"Yes, we do," Chief Walker replies. "We'll keep it short and to the point. We want to know if you saw the driver when the car broke through the Police barricade."

I don't look up. "Yeah, I saw him. That's why I grabbed the boys. I saw that cocksucker gunning for us with his car."

"Did you try to hold onto both boys?" Detective Hill asks.

I can't even raise my head. I nod down at my hands. I can still feel Georgie flying out of my grip. "The car hit me too hard. It tore him away from me."

"Did you see what happened to him after you lost your grip on him?" Chief Walker asks.

"I didn't see anything. I was rolling away too fast. I just tried to cover Dion as much as I could and take the hits myself."

"So you didn't see what Mr. Monroe did after he hit you?"

"No, I didn't see anything. I kept my eyes closed right up until they put me in the ambulance. I was injured, remember?"

"Yeah, we know," Chief Walker replies. "We just want to know what you'll be able to testify about when it comes time to trying this piece of shit."

Something in his tone finally gives me permission to look up at them. At least they realize what a monster the boys' father is.

"I wish I could be more help. Did you catch the guy?"

"He's in jail and he won't be getting bailed out this time," Chief Walker replies. "He's been denied bail, so he'll stay locked up until he goes to trial."

"We didn't have any problem apprehending him at the scene, either, if that's what you're asking," Detective Hill adds. "He didn't even try to flee."

I frown at him. "Really?"

The two cops exchange glances. Something in that look gives me a very bad feeling.

"What is it?" I ask. "What aren't you telling me?"

They look at each other again and Chief Walker sighs. "We weren't sure if we should tell you. Chief Brewer said you were taking Georgie's death really hard and none of us wanted to make it harder for you than it already was."

I cringe. "Tell me what about Georgie's death? Just tell me."

"You're gonna find out either way because we need you to testify against the father." Detective Hill lowers his voice to a hushed undertone exactly the way John did. This can't be good. "The father stopped his car after he hit you. Georgie landed on the pavement next to his mother's car.....and the father backed up three times to run Georgie over three different times to make sure the boy was dead. That's how we apprehended the father. He was still there at the scene. He didn't leave. He would have gone after the rest of you if he got the chance."

I stare down at my hands, but I can't see them. Tears sting my eyes, but I refuse to let them fall in front of these two cops.

They must be able to see my reaction, though. "We'll leave you alone, man," Chief Walker murmurs. "We'll go over your testimony when it comes closer to the time to take the bastard to trial. You go home and heal up. You did everything you could to save Georgie. You should be proud of saving Dion. That's the best thing anyone could d o."

I don't look up when they leave the room. I wait until the door closes and tears streak down my cheeks, but I can't even sob. This is so much worse than I thought—so much worse than ever I dared to fear.

I just sit there staring down at my hands through my tears. The pain in my body doesn't even come close to this crushing sensation in the middle of my chest. I'll never get over this. It will haunt me until my dying day.

I don't know how long I sit there. A nurse snaps me out of my stupor by coming in and fussing around the room. "A friend of yours stopped by earlier and dropped off your truck," she tells me. "It's in the hospital parking lot waiting for you. Here are the keys."

She puts the keys on the bed next to me. I don't even have the energy to ask which friend dropped off my truck.

It could have been anyone from the firehouse. It could have been one of the Brewers or Ellen or Caleb or Ellis. It might even have been Brooke. I wouldn't put it past her.

I can't even appreciate that she's willing to step out of my life to make this easier for me. She came to visit me with the rest of the crew. She doesn't make a big deal about our relationship ending. She'll just go back to the way things were before.

I've never been so grateful to anyone for anything, but not even that makes me feel better.

I pull on my shirt, grit my teeth to put on my shoes, and sign myself out of the hospital. I don't know how I'm going to get back to work. I can barely move.

I wince again when I sit down behind the wheel. The contact between the seat and my back hurts like a bastard. Moving my arms and legs to drive the truck blinds me with pain. I'm a wreck inside and o ut.

I park in front of my house, but I feel even worse when I go inside. Everything here reminds me of Brooke. The coffee table, the kitchen counter, my bedroom, the bathroom, the couch—all those memories slap me in the face.

All the places we didn't do it remind me of all the fantasies of places I wanted to do it with her. I wanted to christen every piece of furniture, every inch of carpet, and every room with her screams of pleasure.

Don't ask me how I'm going to sleep in my own bed without her. I don't want to be alive without her, but I am. I can't even say I'm alive. I might as well not be.

I get back in my truck and drive away. What am I supposed to do—sell my house—the house I worked so hard to build? I could never do that.

I drive out to the beach. I need to be alone where no one will see me feeling sorry for myself.

I get out of the truck and walk down to the beach, but I'm not alone. John, Ellen, their daughter Oakleigh, Keith, Leila, Danny, Emily, and Zeke gather on one side of the beach.

Zeke and Oakleigh run through the waves and kick water on each other. Leila carries baby Leon in a sling wrapped around her chest. Keith hovers close by her side while the adults talk.

I can't go near them. They're family. They're all the family I have, but I can't even lean on them for the support I know I need.

All the adults look up when they see me. I can't go over there, not even to say hello. I feel too rotten and they're all so happy. I need to be alone.

I walk off to a different part of the beach. The headland hides me from them. I can think here.

I sit down on the rocks and stare out at the surf. I don't even know what I'm doing here. I'm hiding from my own house. That's the truth.

Georgie's loss hurts as much here as it does at home. Being there or being here doesn't make a difference.

The memories of my time with Brooke hurt the worst of all. I can't even walk into my house without seeing her everywhere.

I see her naked. I see her in her clothes. I see her falling asleep on the couch with me. I see her getting dressed to go to work. I see her eating her breakfast at my dining room table.

Those memories give me such a peaceful, happy, completed feeling.....and then my world comes crashing down when I remember that she's gone. I pushed her away.

I don't hear anyone come up to me. I try not to jump when John squats down next to me. "You okay?" he asks.

I just shrug without looking at him. I realize how bad that looks when he's trying to take care of me. I finally mutter, "Not really."

"Do you think it would help if you got back to work?"

"I wish I could say it would. I don't know if anything will help—ever again. I might get stuck like this."

He puts his hand on my shoulder and squeezes. The bruises hurt, but that touch actually feels good. It's the one good feeling I've had since this whole disaster started.

"I get it," he tells me and I know it's true. "We all get it. We all have patients like that hidden in our closets. If you're feeling healthy enough to work, the firehouse is the best place for you to find the care you need. You know that."

I look down at my hands. "Yeah, I know."

"I know you don't want to talk to me about what happened with Brooke, so let's just talk about you. You don't have to patch things up with her, but you do need to keep working with her. If you don't want to have a relationship with her, just go back to being friends with her the way you used to be. Things were good for both of you then."

"I know. That's what we're doing."

"Good man." He squeezes me again. "Don't stay out too late, huh? Go home and get some rest."

He walks off and leaves me alone. That conversation didn't change anything—and yet it did. It made it easier.

I never thought anything could, but he's right. The firehouse is the best place for me. It's the only place for me. I just need to go back there to find exactly what I need.

Chapter 24:
Brooke

I push the vacuum cleaner around my apartment, dust the shelves, and put away this week's load of laundry. I iron my uniforms and do all the other chores of keeping my house in some kind of order just this side of utter chaos.

I shouldn't think of it that way. I keep my house clean and running smoothly. I let things slide while I was involved with Billy.

Now I'm getting back on the wagon—now that I have all the time in the world to do it. I'm not spending all my nights at his place.

I find the framed newspaper clipping on the coffee table, but the sight of it only upsets me. Don't ask me why I even keep it. Billy doesn't care. He probably doesn't even know I have it.

Obviously he knows I have it, but he doesn't care that I celebrate his victories. He's too haunted by his own troubles to care what I think.

I stick the frame back in the bookshelf where it was before. I slide it between the books so no one sees it there.

No one ever will see it there because Billy will never come over here again. He'll avoid me like the plague from now on.

I'm just winding up the cord on the vacuum when someone knocks on my door. I don't expect anything other than one of my neighbors.

I freeze when I open the door and see Billy standing outside. "Um...hello," I stammer.

"Would you mind if I come in?" he asks. "I need to talk to you about something."

I stand back to let him in. He still looks terrible with bruises all over his face, neck, and hands.

I didn't know when he would be getting out of the hospital. I thought he might be in there for another week, but he seems fine apart from the bruises—and the cloud hanging over his head.

I can see already that he's just as bowed down by Georgie's death as he was when the crew visited him in the hospital.

He doesn't sit down. He stands across the living room from me and stares at me with a depth of misery I've never seen in anyone. I never would have believed anyone could experience this kind of anguish.

I want to help him or comfort him or.....or something. I can't do that. I can't even go near him now. We aren't even friends anymore.

If we'd never gotten involved, I wouldn't have hesitated to put my arms around him and comfort him through this. Now I can only stand here and gaze at a man completely broken by life.

He raises both hands and lets them slap against his thighs. He turns right and then left again before he finally summons the courage to say what he came here to say.

"I'm....I'm sorry I didn't give you any better explanation for why I broke up with you."

"Is that what you did?" I ask. *"Did* you break up with me? You just stopped talking to me. You never even told me point blank that you *were* breaking up with me."

He swallows hard and looks away before he manages to face me again. "You're right. I should have been more direct about that."

"So.....are we breaking up?"

He takes a deep breath. "I owe it to you to break up with you. I don't want to. I have to do it because it's the right thing for you."

"Why do you think that?" I ask. "Why do you think you have to?"

"Because I'm not the man you think I am. You think I'm some kind of firehouse hero...."

"You are a firehouse hero. You save people's lives every day. You saved my life."

He waves that away. "You don't understand."

"Then why can't you explain it to me?"

He squirms, fights himself back, and straightens up in front of me. "That's why I'm here. I owe you an explanation. That's why I'm here—to give it to you."

"Okay. I'm listening."

He has to take another shaky breath to steady himself. "When I was younger, I got involved with a woman....She was a few years older than me and she already had a kid—a little boy about five years old. I.....I was an asshole to her. I did everything I could to control her. I couldn't control my temper. I used to get in her face and accuse her of running around on me. I......" He shuts his eyes and passes his hand across them. "She and the little boy were scared of me. They used to look at me.....exactly the same way those boys looked at their dad when he showed up drunk and tried to stop you from taking care of their mother."

I stare at him taking all this in. "But.....did you ever actually hurt either of them?"

"What difference does it make? I was young and stupid. I hurt them by scaring them. I threatened her. I took her money and only gave her what I thought she needed so she couldn't leave me. I treated both of them like dirt."

"So what happened?"

He forces himself to look away. "She went behind my back, opened a separate bank account, got her pay deposited into that where I couldn't get it, and then she took her son and disappeared. She vanished out of my life and went somewhere I couldn't find her."

He stands off to one side staring at the carpet. That is one hell of a story, but it suddenly makes so many things make sense.

"So.....so that's why you didn't want to see Leila—because of what happened between her and Damon?"

He nods down at the floor and mumbles under his breath. "I started to hate that part of myself. I worked my ass off to get control of myself so I wouldn't blow up like that again......I just haven't been in a relationship since then. I don't trust myself not to do the same thing."

I can't help taking a step nearer, but I don't dare get near enough to touch him. "But you've never acted that way around me even once. I never would have known if you didn't tell me. I bet no one at the firehouse would have suspected, either. You've never lost your temper...."

"I did!" He spins around and practically yells at me, but he still controls himself. "I lost my temper when that asshole hit me. I could have killed him."

Now it all makes sense. Billy snapped then. That's when everything fell apart.

"But you didn't kill him, Billy," I point out. "You didn't even hit him back. You restrained him so the cops could arrest him and then you were the one who saved Dion. You might have lost your temper, but you controlled it. You used your temper for good. You protected me and the rest of the crew. Think about it. You've never acted controlling around me. You've never threatened me or gotten in my face about other guys."

He turns sideways and looks down at the floor again. "I got jealous and you weren't even mine then.....and I did control you."

"When?"

He tries to shrug it away. He won't look at me. "During sex."

I blink at him trying like anything to understand what the hell he's talking about. "When did you ever control me during sex? You never did anything to me during sex that I didn't want."

He keeps writhing inside his clothes. "You don't know what was going on in my head."

I finally summon the resolve to cross the room and stand next to him. I want to touch him. I want to fold him in my arms and make this all okay.

"Whatever was going on in your head doesn't matter. What matters is how you treated me. You treated me like a gentleman every hour of every day. You never made me feel even marginally uncomfortable—about anything. You made me feel safe and protected and cared for. I could never ask for more than that."

"It isn't good enough," he mutters. "You deserve better. I thought I left all that behind, but that night brought it all back. If I could lose it with him, I might lose it with you. I might slip up...or you might do something I didn't like. I couldn't let that happen to you."

I lower my voice to a murmur. I have to convince him. This is my last chance. If he doesn't get it now, he never will.

"Listen to me, Billy," I breathe. "You aren't responsible for Georgie's death or for Dion getting hurt. You gave them their best chance at survival. You took the hit from that car to save their lives."

He won't raise his face to look at me. "He thought I was moving in on his family. That's why he ran me down. I understand how guys like that think. I saw it written all over his face when he was coming at me in his car."

"Then you understand that he was completely irrational," I point out. "You weren't moving in on his family any more than Josh was touching his wife inappropriately by checking her for injuries. You should understand better than anyone that nothing he thought was based on anything real."

He only shakes his head. "It doesn't matter because you're better off without me. I love you...." He chokes on the words. "I have to protect you. This is the best way I can do that. I'm sorry it didn't work out, but I have to do this. I couldn't live with myself if anything happened to you."

He doesn't wait for me to answer. He walks out the door, closes it behind him, and I hear his truck pull away.

I spend a few more hours cleaning the house, but I can't stop thinking about that conversation and Billy's story.

Whatever he did to that woman and her son, Billy obviously feels terrible about it. He's been beating himself up for however many years it's been since it happened.

Now I understand why he always holds himself back from everything. He doesn't think he deserves success or happiness.

He realizes how badly he screwed up. He does more than realize it. He's been working for years to make sure it doesn't happen again, especially in any relationship.

He's even prepared to live alone for the rest of his life if it means protecting the people he cares about.

Now I know he loves me. I knew before, but now I know just how much. He's willing to walk away because he doesn't trust himself to protect me from himself.

I go over every single living moment I've ever spent with the guy. We worked together for years before this whole relationship started. We've been friends, colleagues, crewmates—family.

I can't remember him ever doing anything dangerous or inappropriate to anyone. The only thing anyone could possibly point to was when he and Andy had a problem with Josh replacing Ellen.

Even then, Billy got over it once he got to know Josh. No one could have a problem with Josh.

Billy took a punch to protect Josh from Carson Monroe. That was the punch that ruined Billy's life.

He never did anything to me. He never acted controlling or dangerous or threatening.

He has never once in all the years I've known him done anything that scared me—ever. I've always felt safe with him—a lot safer than most guys I've dated.

The thing is I always knew he'll do absolutely anything to protect me. He stepped in front of that guy because Carson Monroe shoved me.

Billy Cates is one of the most selfless guys I've ever met. I just wish he could accept some happiness for himself. God knows he's earned it

.

I can't keep this under my hat. I get in my car and wind up driving to the firehouse. Billy won't be there. He isn't back at work yet.

The crew is all out on a call. I'm the only one here.

I go upstairs and stop there to take a deep breath. I can't let the sun go down with all these questions struggling in my head.

I walk over to John's office. The door stands open while he works at his desk.

I tap my knuckles against the door and he looks up. "Hey, stranger!" he greets me. "Come on in and take a seat. What did you want to see me about?"

I shut the door behind me and sit down, but I can't stop shaking. I've been in this office dozens of times for performance reviews, incident reports, and professional development evaluations. None of them comes close to this for pure, nerve-racking anxiety.

I squash my hands between my knees. "I need to ask you......if Billy has a criminal record."

John's jaw drops and his eyes fall out of their sockets. "Excuse me?!" he gasps.

I see right away from his reaction that Billy doesn't have a criminal record. John would know and he wouldn't act so surprised and shocked by my question if Billy had a record.

John straightens out his expression immediately and clears his throat. "I think you already know that's confidential. I wouldn't be able to tell you one way or the other if he did." He frowns at me. "Is there some reason you want to know?"

I try to shrug it off. "You've never seen Billy do anything that would cause concern, have you? I mean, apart from him acting bad-tempered these last few days. Have you? I mean, he's never done anything that would make you think he was unsafe to work on this crew. Have you?"

"No, never." He frowns again. "Have you? Is that what this is about? Did you want to tell me something?"

"No, I've never seen him do anything concerning—ever. I guess that's why I'm asking. I just needed confirmation that I'm not the only one who thinks this."

"Thinks what?" he asks.

"That he's never done anything concerning."

"No, I haven't seen him do anything concerning. As far as I know, no one else on the crew has ever complained about his behavior, either—not that they ever told me about."

I nod. "I thought so. That's what I thought."

He frowns again. "Are you all right? What is this about?"

"Nothing," I lie. "I'm just worried about Billy. These last few days have been hard on him."

"I know. I would have suggested you do something about it, but I guess he doesn't want that."

"No, he doesn't. We're over for real. I know that now."

"That's a shame. You two were good for each other."

"I thought so, too, but apparently Billy doesn't think so."

He makes a face. "Far be it for me to tell a man how to live his life, but that's just BS. Just saying."

I try not to grin at him. "Thanks, John. I really appreciate you saying that."

He smiles back at me and I get out of his office with as much of my dignity intact as I can. He didn't tell me anything I didn't already know, but it sure is nice to hear it from someone I trust.

Chapter 25: Billy

I roll up to my first shift back at the firehouse. The whole place erupts in cheers the minute I walk in.

The guys whistle, hoot, and clap. I feel my cheeks burning, but I can't help grinning. This feels good. At least someone is happy to see me.

Brooke is working today, too, and she won't stop grinning, hollering, and clapping with the others. She bursts out laughing at my reaction.

Ellis shoves Josh in the shoulder. "Stand aside, Batman. There's a new superhero in town."

"That dude beat me hands down," Josh replies. "I'm just an adoring bystander compared to him."

I can't stop blushing. My stomach hurts, this feels so good. "Thanks, guys."

Keith pats me on the back. "It's good to have you back, big guy. The place wasn't the same without you."

"You better watch out, Keith," Caleb tells him. "Billy can drive a mean rescue truck when you aren't around."

"Shut the hell up," I counter. "He'll always drive. I'm just the substitute."

"Hell, you can fly to the calls in your bright red cape with a big blue S sewn onto the front of your outfit," Brooke tells me. "You don't have to ride in the truck at all."

The others all burst out laughing again and I find myself grinning at her. There are no hard feelings anymore.

I knew there wouldn't be, but it sure is nice to hear her joining in and welcoming me back. I....

I stop myself from thinking I love her for that. She's just a friend now. That's all she'll ever be.

The group breaks up and we get to work on our jobs. The morning passes in the usual way and we go up to the break room before our first call.

"Another car crash on the highway!" I read on the dispatch notes as the truck pulls out. "It's a big rig crashed down an embankment. No casualties!"

"Now you're talking!" Ellis calls from the back.

"If there are no casualties, what are we doing here?" Danny asks.

"Take it up with the manager," I yell over my shoulder.

We don't have time to talk before we pull up to the call. I find myself checking in all directions to make sure the scene is secure, but no one comes.

Carson Monroe is in jail and he'll stay there. He's facing one count of aggravated vehicular homicide, two counts of attempted vehicular homicide, another four counts of regular attempted murder, arson, and a boatload of other charges. He won't be coming after me again—not on this call.

I almost dread what I'll find on this call, but as soon as we get out of the truck, we can all see what caused the crash.

The truck in question lies on its side down the steep embankment. All its tires point up at the sky where we can see them. One of them is completely blown out and barely hanging onto the rim.

"It looks like his tire blew and that's why he drove off the road," Brooke remarks.

"That's the driver over there," one of the Police officers tells us. "He climbed out on his own. He isn't hurt."

"Someone is finally taking my suggestions into account," Ellis replies and a few people laugh.

"So what do you want us to do?" Danny asks. "It looks like the scene is secure."

The officer opens his mouth to answer, but right then, a deafening ka-boom rocks the landscape as the whole truck explodes. The noise and shockwave of outward bursting fire makes us all duck, but this time, the fire doesn't put anyone in danger.

"That's why you're here!" the officer yells over the noise. "The gas tank punctured. It's been leaking since the crash."

"Nothing will put out a gas fire like that," Keith points out. "Just let it burn."

"You'll stick around and make sure it doesn't spread, won't you?" the officer asks. "We got rubberneckers backed up for ten miles. The last thing we need is the fire creeping up on the highway."

"We'll keep an eye on it," Keith replies. "No problem."

He waits until the cops go back to directing traffic. "Now all we need is some marshmallows," Ellis murmurs so no one outside our crew overhears him.

The others laugh and Keith sends the ambulances back to the firehouse. Keith, Danny, Ellis, Caleb, Brooke, Josh, and I settle down to watch and wait. We have nothing left to do but make sure the fire doesn't spread.

It isn't in any danger of doing that. All the grass on the embankment is green, damp, and lush. It won't catch fire, and if it does, it won't spread.

"If we get another more urgent call, we're leaving," Keith snarls after an hour. "This is for the birds."

We wait another hour before he gets a call from John to come back to the firehouse. We've been gone almost the entire morning with no sign that the truck fire is going to die down.

We drive back and put our gear away. "Who wants to take bets on what our next call will be?" Ellis asked.

"This is a firehouse, not a casino," Keith tells him. "We aren't taking bets on calls."

"Why not?" Ellis asked. "What else do we have to do with our free time?"

"Next thing I know, you'll be taking bets on how many patients we'll have and what their injuries will be," Keith counters. "Have some respect for the job, man."

Josh starts to say, "If you need something to do, you could...."

He breaks off when another car pulls into the driveway. It parks in front of the trucks and blocks them in, too, but this isn't a cop who should know better.

Dead silence falls over the crew and my stomach turns a somersault when Sadie Monroe gets out of her car with Finn and Dion.

She lets the boys out of the car, picks up Finn, and takes Dion's hand before they all walk in.

I thought I was putting my life back together, but seeing these people brings it all back.

Sadie looks like a wet dishrag. Dark shadows ring her swollen, bloodshot eyes and her lips keep spasming.

She pulls up in front of the crew, but she can't get her mouth to obey her to speak.

Dion speaks first. "Hi, Billy," he tells me.

"Hey, buddy," I choke. "You okay?"

He nods. "Are you?"

"I'm all right," I tell him. "I'm glad you're okay. I was worried about you."

Keith interrupts. "What can we do for you, Ma'am?"

"Um....I was wondering...." Sadie's eyes skip around the group. She falls apart again when she looks at me. "We were wondering....Billy....We're having Georgie's funeral this weekend. We'd all appreciate it if you could come."

I shift my weight to my other foot. The whole crew stands in silence listening to this. "I don't know if that's a good idea, Ma'am," I husk. "I didn't really do anything..."

"It would mean a lot....to all of us....if you were there." She can barely get her voice to function.

"Please come, Billy," Dion interjects. "Please?"

"You're very special to all of us, Billy," Sadie stammers again and chokes on sobs. "We really hope you'll make it. It's at Greenhill Cemetery, Saturday at three PM."

I don't know what to say. Going to Georgie's funeral sounds like a trip through Hell itself. It would kill me to face all that agony all over again.

"Please come," she insists. "That's all I'll say. Sorry to bother all of you. We'll just leave now."

She turns to leave. Dion hangs back and says, "Bye, Billy."

I can barely speak to say, "Bye," before they get in their car and leave.

None of the crew says a word. They drift away one by one and get back to work. In a few minutes, they start talking in low tones that eventually come back to normal volume. No one mentions Sadie's invitation.

I try to put it out of my mind. Saturday is a long way off. I have enough to deal with just getting back on the job.

I waste a few hours helping Caleb and Drew change a tire on one of the ambulances. "Come on, Superman! Just lift the ambulance so we can change it," Caleb teases. "We don't need to use the jack."

"Shut up, man," I chide. "Leave me alone already."

He grins at me, but pretty soon, it's time to go home.

I'm just getting into my truck when Brooke comes over to me. "Hey," she greets me.

"Hey," I reply.

"Listen. I don't know if you planned to go to Georgie's funeral....."

"I wasn't planning on it. It's real nice that they invited me, but it's hard enough dealing with it without having the funeral shove it in my face."

"I understand," she replies. "I just wanted to let you know that, if you did want to go, I'd be happy to go with you—as a support person. Then you wouldn't have to go alone. It might mean a lot to you to be around people who are as broken up over Georgie's death as you are. It might make you realize you aren't carrying around this grief alone. Other people feel the same way. Anyway, the offer is there if you want it. Let me know if you want me to go with you."

She turns away to her car. She really would just drop that there and leave without waiting for me to answer.

Now I know she really means it. She doesn't offer in some under-handed attempt to get back into my life. She just wants to help me.

As soon as she says it, I know I have to go. I have to be with Georgie's family—and I need them to be with me. I need to do something to bury him—literally and figuratively.

I need to be around people who are grieving over him the same way I am. How touching that Brooke of all people realizes that.

She also realizes how much harder it would be for me to go alone. She knows I need someone in my corner.

"Brooke!" I call after her.

She turns around and looks up at me with a perfectly neutral expression. She really would let our whole relationship go and never say anything about it—for me. She'll do it to give me some peace of mind.

"Thank you," I tell her.

She smiles at me and pulls her keys out of her pocket. "I'll see you Saturday."

Chapter 26: Brooke

I run down the stairs of my apartment building when I see Billy pull his truck into the parking lot. He gets out and opens the passenger door for me, but he doesn't smile the way he used to. He doesn't even look at me.

He wears black jeans, black leather boots, and a black T-shirt under his black leather jacket. He looks casual, but ready for a funeral.

I wear a knee-length black dress, black pantyhose, and black ballet flats. I wear my hair down with no jewelry. We're going to a funeral. We aren't here to enjoy ourselves.

I stop in front of Billy and squeeze his arm. "You okay?"

He nods down at the pavement and doesn't look at me. He's a million miles away.

I get into the truck and he shuts the door before we drive to Greenhill Cemetery. A bunch of mourners are already there, including Sadie and the two surviving boys.

Dion breaks away from his mother, comes right over to us, grabs Billy's hand, and tows him forward. "Billy! You come stand with us."

Dion drags Billy away from me and over to his mother and little brother. Dion doesn't let go of Billy's hand. The boy parks Billy right next to the family in front of the grave.

The miniature coffin rests on a stand over the hole with a pile of dirt to one side. Flowers cover the casket and surround the grave.

The other mourners mill around murmuring to each other, hugging, and occasionally crying.

I stand back out of the way. This isn't about me. I'm just here to support Billy.

Sadie comes straight over to him and holds out her arms to hug him. "Thank you so much for coming!" She holds him at arm's length and gazes at him with tears streaming down her cheeks. "Thank you....for Dion's life.....and thank you for everything you've done for our family. None of us can thank you enough."

He mumbles under his breath. "Thank you for having me, Ma'am. I'm just doing what I can."

She's just letting go of him when an older couple comes over. They're also sobbing their eyes out, especially the man.

He grips Billy by both shoulders in a tight hold that probably hurts Billy's injuries. He doesn't even flinch, though.

"You're the man who saved Dion, aren't you?" the old guy tells Billy. "I'm Dion's and Georgie's grandfather, Malcolm Witherspoon....and this is my wife, Colleen. We're both so grateful to you—for everything you've done."

"Thank you, Sir," Billy mumbles. "You're too kind."

"Not at all, not at all," Malcolm exclaims. "We're all so grateful you could come. You being here means the world to us."

I can see all this attention making Billy uncomfortable, so I take a chance and walk over to him.

I'm just taking my place next to him when Sadie notices me. She gasps and her eyes fly open. "You're here, too!"

"I'm here to support Billy," I tell her. "We're friends...."

"From the firehouse! I remember!" She grabs my hand. "You're the one who got us out of the burning house. I could never forget."

I turn bright red, but she won't leave me alone. She turns to the two grandparents. They must be her parents. "This is the paramedic who found us during the house fire." She turns back to me talking fast. "I'm so grateful you could come! Thank you so much for saving all of us! I don't know what to say."

I don't know what to say, either, but just then, another four people come over and start making a fuss over Billy. They all talk nonstop about how he saved Dion, pulled both boys from the wrecked car, and took the hit when Carson Monroe's car plowed into them.

I get forgotten in the scuffle, but I don't leave Billy's side. He gets mobbed by mourners all thanking him, hugging him, and expressing how much they admire him.

I get pushed to the side, but I'm glad. He needs this. He needs to see exactly what he's done.

So many of his patients must have families like this—people who owe him their lives for things he's done for their loved ones. I only hope he realizes now just how many lives he's touched.

The minister shows up a few minutes later and everyone returns to their seats. Dion grabs Billy's hand. "You sit down here, Billy."

Dion pulls Billy into a seat right next to the family. Dion positions Billy at the end of the family row, at the far end from Sadie and the two boys.

Sadie's parents sit on Billy's other side.

I stand in the back where no one will see me. I don't want to intrude on this moment between Billy and the family. Today is all about him.

The minister launches into a speech about God's grace and how Georgie got taken from us before his time. The minister talks about the innocence of childhood and the blessing of God's mercy—whatever that means.

The minister goes on at length. I'm not even sure anymore what the guy is talking about, but it doesn't even seem to matter.

Billy stares at Georgie's coffin. I can't tell from here what reaction Billy might be having. Is he finally getting it? Does he finally see that he isn't the monster he thinks he is?

I barely listen to the minister's words. The coffin and everything else vanishes in the tears welling up in my eyes.

I can finally cry—not just for Georgie, but for all the patients I've lost over the years. I can bury them all today. I just hope Billy can do the same thing.

All the mourners start crying when the stand lowers the coffin into the hole. Then everyone comes forward one person after another to throw dirt from the pile onto the coffin.

Dion, Finn, Sadie, and the grandparents do it one after another. Everyone comes forward to pay their last respects.

Billy sits in one place without moving until the very end. He shows no emotion. He just stares down into that hole.

I'm just starting to think he might skip it when he stands up. No one goes near him or says anything while he stands at the hole staring for a long time.

He finally picks up a handful of dirt and throws it in. He croaks under his breath, "Bye, Georgie."

Sadie rushes him, slips her hand through his arm, and rests her head on his shoulder sobbing hard. Dion approaches Billy on his other side and sneaks his hand into Billy's.

The three of them stand there together in a halo of…..something I can't define. I can't call it happiness or even peace. I don't know if any of them will ever be happy or peaceful again.

I can only call that halo love. It's the glow of love—love for Georgie, love for each other, love for something we can only get from each other.

At some unseen signal, all the mourners turn away. The little family breaks apart and everyone goes through another series of hugging, crying, talking, and supporting each other.

I go over to Billy in the crowd, but he's too busy hugging everyone else. Everyone thanks him for coming and again for saving Dion and all the help he's given their family.

No one says anything to me and that's the way it should be. I'm only here for him. I don't need recognition for anything—not the way he does.

Sadie finally clasps his hands. She hasn't stopped crying since Billy showed up. "We'd like to invite you over for dinner sometime," she tells him. "We'd love to have you. I don't want us to be strangers after this."

"I'd like that," he growls. "Thank you for everything. Thank you for inviting me."

Dion says, "Bye, Billy."

Billy rumples his hair. "I think you mean, 'see ya later', pal. We'll see each other around sometime."

Dion starts to smile. "Yeah."

"You boys take care of your mother."

"We will," Dion replies.

Billy starts to smile, too, but he holds himself back and then the grandparents come over to talk to Billy, too.

They're in the middle of their conversation when someone screams from the back of the crowd. I barely have time to glance over my shoulder before a younger man shoves his way into the group.

I freeze when I think it might be Carson Monroe coming back, but he can't come back. He's in jail.

This man looks similar, but he's shorter and thicker set in the shoulders. He pushes the mourners out of the way, storms up to Sadie, and gets in her face.

"What's this bullshit about you making accusations against my brother? Huh?" he demands.

Sadie's eyes dart in all directions. She tries her best to avoid looking at the guy. He must be Carson's brother. "I never told anyone anything, Felix. I was just trying to...."

"How dare you?!" Felix snaps. "He gave you everything and this is how you repay him? You got some nerve. It's your fault he's in jail right now because you're out here smearing his name with your lies."

Billy steps forward and sticks his arm between Sadie and Felix. "Hey, pal. Take a step back. Whatever your beef is with her, this isn't the time or the place."

Felix smacks Billy's arm out of the way and rounds on him. "Who the hell are you, *pal?* Are you the guy she's been sleeping around with? Huh? My brother always knew she was a tramp from the wrong side of town, but this is going too far—inviting *you* to my nephew's funeral."

Billy only sighs. "I'm the guy that tried to save your nephew's life, *pal*—you know, your nephew who's lying in his grave right now because your dirtbag brother ran him over with his car—and then backed up and ran him over with his car three more times just to make sure the kid was deader than dead? Is that the guy we're talking about? I can promise you Sadie didn't make any accusations against your brother about that. She had nothing to do with him getting arrested for that—or for running *me* down in his car for trying to save his sons' lives. The forty Police officers, firefighters, and emergency medical staff who witnessed the incident are the ones who testified against your brother—not her."

"You don't know what the hell you're talking about," Felix snaps.

"Oh, I think I do," Billy replies. "I was there. You weren't. Who told you Sadie made the accusation—your brother? He's out of his mind—but you already knew that. He was probably so drunk he doesn't even remember it."

Felix storms up to him and chest-bumps Billy. Billy stands six inches taller and outweighs Felix by fifty pounds at least, but Billy lets Felix knock him one step backward.

"You better stay away from my family, asshole," Felix snaps.

"Or what?" Billy asks. "What are you gonna do if I don't?"

Felix opens his mouth to say something else, but one of the mourners must have called the Police. A couple of uniformed officers push through the crowd and flank Felix on both sides. They try to take hold of his arms. "Excuse me, Sir...." one of the officers begins.

He spins around and swings his arm at them, too. They dodge, close on him in a combined tackle, and bring him to the ground.

Billy stands off to one side watching. Felix kicks and struggles. He keeps yelling curses and threats even as the officers haul him away and shove him into their squad car.

The other mourners go back to whispering and commenting to each other, but Billy doesn't rejoin them. He says one last quick goodbye to Sadie and her sons before he nods at me and walks away.

Chapter 27: Brooke

Billy leaves the funeral, but he doesn't leave the cemetery. He walks more and more slowly as we cross the lawns.

"You okay?" I finally ask.

He stops out of sight of the funeral, but we're nowhere near his truck.

He doesn't face me. He gazes across the sunny lawns lying warm and glowing in the breeze. "Yeah, I'm okay," he murmurs. "You were right. I needed this."

I take a chance and compress his arm. "I'm really proud of the way you handled that. You kept your composure perfectly. You didn't let that guy push your buttons at all."

He finally turns around and locks his eyes on me. "You were right about that, too. I'm nothing like him."

I burst into a grin. I can't believe the look of relief and actual clarity in his eyes. "You aren't. I told you. You're one of the good guys."

He starts grinning. "Yeah. I am. I didn't see it before. I needed all those people to show me."

I can't stop beaming at him. "I'm so happy for you. You earned this."

He bursts out in one laugh and bites it back. "Let's get out of here."

We head back to the truck, but we skirt the funeral so he doesn't get caught up with all the mourners trying to talk to him again.

"Do you think you'll see Sadie and her family again?" I ask on our way there.

"Why not? It will be good to keep an eye on the boys. They'll need a positive male role model in their lives—someone who can show them there's another way to be a man than just being an arrogant, violent asshole."

"You would be perfect for that." I squeeze his arm again. I have to stop doing that, but I'm so happy for Billy that I don't seem to be able to stop.

I don't care about our relationship ending if we can just get this back—this easy friendship and mutual support. I don't care about anything as long as he's happy and content with himself and his life.

He opens the passenger door for me, I get in, and he drives across town. I gaze out the window thinking about everything that's happened. I don't need to worry about anything anymore. Everything is all right and back to the way it should be.

I come to my senses when Billy pulls into the driveway—in front of his house. I jolt upright. "What are we doing here? I thought you were taking me home."

He turns in the seat to face me....and like some kind of miracle from Heaven, he slips his fingers into mine. "Stay here, Brooke. I don't want you to go anywhere else. This house isn't what it used to be without you. I need you here. Come inside....and stay here."

I stare at him with my mouth open. "You mean it?"

He bursts into another beautiful, glowing smile. "Yeah. I mean it. I can't stand this place without you. I don't ever want you to leave—unless you have to work. Come on. Say you'll stay with me."

"I...." I gulp to get my voice working. I don't know what to say.

I could ask how I know he won't have another episode of doubting himself, but the radiant sunshine beaming out of his face tells me all I need to know.

He gets out, opens the passenger door for me, and takes my hand to lead me inside.

I can't believe I'm actually back here....and he's asking me to stay. I don't have to ask what changed.

Nothing changed between us. There was never anything wrong between us. The only thing wrong was inside Billy's head and heart. He couldn't shake off his past, but now the cloud lifts and the sun comes out. He's free.

He stops me in the living room, puts his keys on the kitchen counter, and shuts the front door. I look around his house. I know everything in this place. I know everything that will happen between us. This place holds no secrets for me anymore.

He doesn't hold any secrets for me anymore, either. I can read everything in his eyes. His past lies bare for me to see.

It will never haunt him again. His past is the reason he cares so much and works so hard to help people. His past is the reason he saved Dion. Billy wouldn't have been able to do that if he hadn't gone through all that horror before.

He takes a step toward me and I take a step toward him. I start grinning and then he does the same thing. "So...." he begins. "Where should be do it first?"

I burst out laughing. "Where did you have in mind?"

"Well...as it happens....I have a list...."

My eyes pop out. "A list? You have a list?"

"Well, not so much a list as well.....everything."

I frown. "Huh? I don't understand."

He waves that away still bushing to his eyelashes. "Never mind. It's just something stupid going on in my head."

"Tell me."

"Well...over there...." He points to the coffee table. "Over there is where you interrupted my fajita lunch by jumping me."

"I jumped *you!*" I counter. "You're the one who jumped me in the hall that first night."

He laughs. "Okay. You got me there."

"So...." I look around the house with new eyes. "So is everything on the list?"

"Pretty much." He starts laughing and his cheeks color even more.

I glance around....and then I see it. Every piece of furniture, every inch of carpet, every room, the deck, the hot tub, the garden—each one offers an unlimited selection of positions, delights, possibilities, and experiences. How can I choose just one?

Billy interrupts my thoughts. "Okay, too many choices. I have a better idea. Come with me."

He takes my hand and leads me down the hall to his bedroom. It's as neat and orderly as always. The guy sure knows how to take care of his house.

He stops me by the bed and his eyes drill into me as never before. I see my future in those eyes.

He holds me captive by my eyes while he tugs my dress over my head and slowly, deliberately takes off his jacket. He throws my dress aside and kisses me deeply, passionately, longingly.....and expertly.

I stand before him in my bra and panties. My desire for him erupts. He'll undress me, lay me down on that bed, take his clothes off, and carry me to the stars.

He'll explore every inch of my body with his hands and mouth. He'll claim every forgotten recess as his own and wring all the pleasure from each of those parts that can possibly be wrung from them.

He'll find new ways to bring me to screaming ecstasy until I crumble in his arms. He'll find ways to bring me to screaming ecstasy that not even I have thought of yet.

He'll discover my body, my mind, and my soul the same way he'll discover the hidden sensuality and erotic wildness of every corner of his house, garden, yard, and deck.

This house was made for the journey in front of us. Some part of him knew way back then and he's been building this for us all this time.

We'll collapse panting and breathless but still electrified for each other. We'll sleep in this bed. He'll crawl on top of me, push between my legs, and fill me with every part of himself.

He'll crawl into my mind and heart the same way. He'll become so much a part of me that I won't remember who I was before.

Then all those years I lived without him will fade like a distant nightmare. Only this bright future will remain when we call each other our own and this house our home—exactly the way it should be.

<u>End of Book 5.</u>

Keep Reading

F irehouse Blues Series: Book 6: Fallen Hero

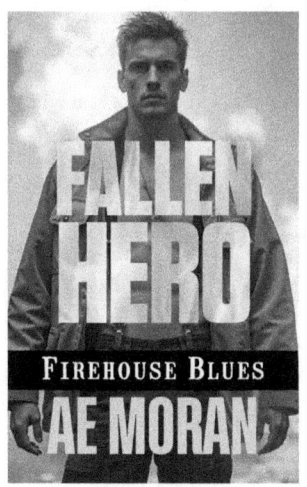

Paramedic Sophie McNish is just as pissed off and defensive as the rest of the Howe Firehouse crew when Fire Chief John Brewer tells everyone that the firehouse is getting a health and safety review. The crew has had too many dangerous incidents recently leaving multiple crew members injured, patients dead, and paramedic Ellen Foreman permanently disabled.

No one wants to cooperate with the investigation, but the crew can only stare in stunned shock when they meet their new health and safety officer. Carter Holt is severely burned over most of his head and body and he looks hideous.

He wins the crew over by explaining that he became a Fire Service health and safety officer to ensure the safety and wellbeing of his fellow firefighters. He's only here to make sure they get the working conditions they deserve.

Everything blows up when Sophie develops an instant connection with Carter. He distances himself from her, but not before her ex-boyfriend firefighter Andy Skinner notices.

Andy doesn't want to accept that Sophie might have feelings for someone else. When Andy doesn't get his way, his obsessive need to retaliate against Carter will backfire in ways that devastate the whole fire crew.

Can Sophie ever find happiness when the Fire Department's greatest hero falls to a madman and leaves the crew broken and ruined?

You can find it at your favorite book retailer.

Get All of AE Moran's Free Books

S ign Up Once—Get all A.E. Moran's free books including brand new releases

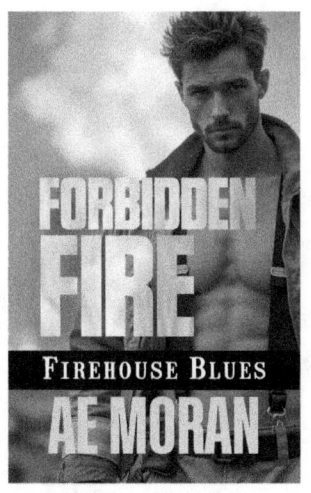

When what you want most is the one thing you can never have......

Austin McAuliffe is every woman's dream firefighter—young, strong, drop-dead hot, and selflessly dedicated to his career—and to the woman of his heart, Emma Brady. Only one other person holds a place in Austin's life—his best friend and fellow firefighter, Theo Gough. Austin insists on Theo spending time with Austin and Emma as a couple, especially when these two firefighters have a hard day at the office.

No one can believe when Austin completely flips out and randomly accuses Theo and Emma of flirting with each other in front of the whole fire crew. Could there be some deeper, more sinister reason for Austin to suddenly lose his mind and lash out at those closest to him?

Emma is devastated when Austin coldly dumps her with no warning and disappears out of her life, but Austin casts a long shadow. The nightmare of his sudden betrayal will come back to haunt Emma and Theo long after Austin is gone. Will the ghosts of the past ruin any chance for them to regain their happiness.....or will Austin's madness take down everyone he cares about along with him?

Sign up at www.authoraemoran.com to read it for free.

About AE Moran

A .E Moran is the contemporary romance pen name for Theo Mann.

I write 70 books per year—and yes, before you ask, all these books are my original creative work. Nothing written under my name is AI-generated or ghostwritten because I write better than AI and any ghostwriter out there.

People don't read fiction for entertainment or to escape from reality. People read fiction to see their humanity reflected in another person's character and story.

This is my promise to you. When you read my books, you'll see your own humanity reflected in the characters and stories. I take this commitment to my readers very seriously. My books are an intimate form of communication between us. I would never disrespect my readers by turning that over to a machine or another writer. This is my bond between me and you as my reader.

I write 20,000 words per day as my daily work output. If anyone with a public platform would like to challenge me to prove this in a controlled environment, feel free to contact me on this website's contact page.

I worked as a professional ghostwriter for fifteen years. Now I'm going for the Guinness World Record by writing 700 books over the next ten years and 1400 books over the next twenty years, all originally written by me. See my website for the full book list.

I'm also the author of *Proof for the Existence of God* and the *Crimes Against Fiction* blog. You can find all my nonfiction work at www.crimes-against-fiction.com.

If you have a story idea, or if you would like me to explore a series in more depth, or if you'd like me to explore a character by writing a spinoff series about that character or world, leave me a message on my website's contact page. I answer all reader emails, so ask me anything, tell me what you liked and didn't like, and let me know where you'd like your favorite series to go. I would love to hear your ideas and find out what you'd like to read next.

You can find out more at www.theomann.com or at www.authoraemoran.com.

Also by AE Moran (so far)

Standalone Novels

Heart on a Knife Edge

Dream Dimension

Just Friends

Back From the Dead

Damaged

Small Town Reunion

Series

Firehouse Blues (Books 1-10)

Turning Point Ranch (Books 1-10)

The Billionaires' Club (Books 1-10)

www.ingramcontent.com/pod-product-compliance
Lightning Source LLC
Chambersburg PA
CBHW070112030726
47506CB00002B/702